Jock Tamson's Legacy

JOCK TAMSON'S LEGACY

Mick McCluskey
WITH ILLUSTRATIONS BY
Belinda Langlands

Intro2 Publishing

COPYRIGHT NOTICE

ABOUT THE AUTHOR

Scottish Musician, Filmmaker, and Best-selling Author Mick McCluskey studied creative writing at The City Lit in London and graduated from the Scottish Film and Television School with a master's degree in film and television production, specializing in Screenwriting and Directing.

Expanding his work to include stage, books, and film & TV production, he has written and directed Drama, Music Documentary, and Animation films, with two of his films having enjoyed cinema release. He also spent thousands of happy hours as a freelance video camera operator working on everything from human embryos to football cup finals.

For half his lifetime Mick has lived in the Sidlaw Hills to the north of the river Tay, preferring to venture out of the tranquillity of his Glen only when he really needs to.
He's a self-confessed workaholic who loves everything life has to offer.

BY THE SAME AUTHOR

Dundonian for Beginners (Mainstream Publishing & Intro2 Publishing)
The Scheme-Hoppers Survival Guide (Mainstream Publishing)
Who Wants to Be a Dundonian? (Black & White Publishing)

ACKNOWLEDGEMENT

Thanks to Croy Langlands, Kevin Murray, Sarah Dalgarno, Alex Benckendorff and Stan Urban, for their help during the production of this book. Nice One Guys!

This book is dedicated to Chinkabile (John) Shanyinde.

Charlie's a taxi-driving money junkie who hates Friday nights. Tonight would be different, he could feel it in his water.

Ella's knee is a supernatural version of the pony express, except that it only brings bad news. Sometimes tragic news. And this time, Ella felt tragic.

With a belly-full of home-made whisky, Robbie prepares for manhood by following his family tradition of shooting at least one trespassing townie before his mum and dad get home from the pub.

The BMW was on autopilot. Jackie was on the horn. Luckily, he was still on the right side of consciousness. Just. He was having a ninety-four miles per hour identity crisis.

Who exactly was Jock Tamson? And what is his Legacy?

This Comic tragedy of errors will reveal all.

Friday nights may never be the same again. And that's a fact.

CONTENTS

CHAPTER 1

IT AIN'T NO WAY TO TREAT A KARAOKE

Alfie and Mary love doing it. They've been doing it together for a long time now and they still love it!

The first time Alfie laid eyes on Mary was in Chambers pub, and she was doing it with 'Drew Larg and the Buzzards'. She was red-hot and having a great time. So was Alfie. He couldn't take his eyes off her. And her voice... Oh what a voice! She was only eighteen, yet she possessed a mature singing voice that had quality firmly stamped all over it. Alfie was gob-smacked and fell arse over elbow in love with her on the spot.

GOB-SMACKED

Mary had been singing soul for as long as she could remember. It was just something she loved doing. It was in her soul. Her parents record collection supplied the lyrics, and with Drew Larg's Buzzards supplying some powerful soul music, her emotions easily did the rest. Mary was well into the second verse of 'The lonely heart and lonely eyes of lonely me', when she first became aware of Alfie. He was staring right at her and singing along. It was plain to see that he was swept up in the emotion of the song, and she was slightly curious to know if he was just a fan of Gladys Knight and the Pips, or did he have real soul in his veins?

JOCK TAMSON'S LEGACY

Alfie had plenty of soul. And plenty bottle. He fancied Mary and he made a play for her. He used a Marvin Gaye song to help him get his point across in not so many words and the band were willing to help. He belted out 'Little darling' with enough passion to make Mary's nipples throb, and by the end of the night, he felt like Marvin Gaye, and she felt like Tammi Terrell as they sang, 'Ain't nothing like the real thing' all the way home in the taxi.

Alfie was the proud owner of a cracking good Karaoke machine, and it didn't take very long for him and Mary to team-up and do a double act on the pub circuit. They called themselves 'Soul Lovers Karaoke Kruise' and after only a few weeks had a diary full of regular bookings and a swelling bank account.

They also had a regular following of soul lovers who would turn up at their gigs. Some would get up and sing, some would be content just to listen and get pished on a cocktail of lager and Tamla Motown.

When Chic first moved from Aberdeen to Dundee it took a while for him to get to know people. The only time he would venture out of his B&B was to go to the pub at the end of his road when Mary and Alfie were doing a gig there. For a few weeks, Chic was content to be a listener, then one night he cracked. He got up on stage and just stood there motionless until the punters quietened down. When they did, they stayed quiet and listened to Chic belt out a heart-wrenching version of 'Sitting on the dock of the bay'.

IT AIN'T NO WAY TO TREAT A KARAOKE

Chic captured a few hearts that night, but the heart that he captured the most was Lillian's, and she was more than willing to declare 'Endless love' in a duet with Chic before the night was out.

Chic and Lillian hit it off pretty well and soon became regular followers of 'Soul Lovers Karaoke Kruise' along with many other people.

Alfie and Mary weren't big on conversation. They communicated through songs, not just to each other, but to other people too.

Mary noticed that whenever some girl would give Alfie the eye, he would normally respond by singing 'Hey girl don't bother me', and that would usually make Mary feel secure in their relationship, but the Christmas Eve gig in the Balmore Bar was different. She felt different.

Alfie felt different too. He'd had eight bacardies and that gave him a dose of the bravados. He'd spent most of the evening leering at Lillian's cleavage out of the corner of his eye and now he was going for it. He blatantly enticed Lillian up for a solo turn (making a real twat of himself, in Mary's opinion) by staring into her eyes and singing, 'Get up (I feel like being a) sex machine'.

Lillian was game for it. She responded by doing a Carla Thomas number called, 'I like what you're doing to me'.

Chic was shattered. He never saw it coming. He hadn't read the signs. And now, there she was, the love of his life, up on stage letting everybody see her for the tart that she was. He was heart-broken.

That night, Chic sang only one song, and it was sung in his head while he lay awake in his kip. It was the Miracles' version of 'Gotta dance to keep from crying'. The lyrics never worked, and Chic sobbed himself to sleep.

By the time Hogmanay came around tongues were already beginning to wag, and Mary's friend Jan thought it her duty to point things out to Mary. The gig had only just started when Jan went on stage and sang number 211 for her friend. It was 'Playboy' by the Marvelettes, and she was singing it to let everybody know what a roving bastard Alfie was.

Sean McNeil was a regular. He was also a stirring little shite, and he was up next. He sang, 'Who's making love (to your old lady while you're out making love)'.

IT AIN'T NO WAY TO TREAT A KARAOKE

That was enough for Mary. She'd been having thoughts of her own on the subject of Alfie's infidelity. Tonight, she would do something about it. She hit the stage with a mind to show the pair of them up, and she sang, 'Mr Big Stuff', much to the dismay of Alfie, and 'Woman to Woman' much to the dismay of Lillian.

The crowd loved it. Especially the ones who had been to the Christmas Eve gig and were privy to all the gossip about the goings-on with Alfie and Lillian.

Alfie was well pissed off. He responded by doing a Billy Ocean number for Lillian just to spite everybody. When the going gets tough, the tough certainly do get going.

The first set was hotting up nicely.

Lillian wasn't a great singer by any standard, but she certainly knew how to pick a song. She picked number 36 and in so doing, she basically told everybody 'I'll be the other woman'.

Alfie was ecstatic. So ecstatic that his next number couldn't be anything other than, 'Hitch Hike'.

Mary was livid. She was finally seeing Alfie as the swine that he really was, and with more than a little encouragement from Jan, she rounded off the first set with the Mary Wells number, 'Drop in the bucket'.

During the break the bar-staff were inundated with punters

ordering drinks and placing side bets as to how the evening would end up.

In the dressing-room come beer-cellar, Mary and Alfie had words. Real words. The cards were laid on the table face up and hiding nothing. They would keep the business together but do it apart. He was moving out and that was that.

As Mary got on stage to open the last set, the crowd hushed, and quiet anticipation set in. She picked the Martha Reeves and the Vandellas' song, 'I'll have to let him go' to break the news to her friends and followers, and someone at the back of the pub broke into tears.

Chic decided to go up next and tell his version of events with the assistance of Daryl Hall and John Oates. He sang, 'She's gone' with the realism of a defeated man. A man who was heartbroken and wasn't afraid to share it.

By the end of the number, you could almost smell the oestrogen in the air as the maternal instincts of most of the female customers flowed out towards their men.

It was all getting out of order. The bar was beginning to sell more tissues than drinks, and the manager of the pub had lost a significant amount of money because of the daft side bets. He wasn't pleased at all with the way the night was going, and he tried to call a halt to the proceedings when he stepped on stage and sang the James Brown classic, 'It's too funky in here'.

IT AIN'T NO WAY TO TREAT A KARAOKE

As the months went on, the situation grew worse. Salt was being rubbed into the open wounds of broken hearts. Alfie took to singing 'What more could a boy ask for', and Lillian took to singing 'Heat wave', to let all the girls know just how virile Alfie was.

From time to time, Chic would get up and sing 'Love you like a brother' just to let newcomers in on the fact that he made a play for Mary a while ago and received a knock-back.

Mary took to singing 'This old heart of mine (is weak for you)'. She still loved Alfie, and she wasn't afraid to sing it. She also told him in not so many words when they would do a duet to 'Private number'.

Jan didn't like seeing her friend crawling to that scumbag Alfie. She was all for Mary striking out and having a shag but not with that git. If she caught sight of Mary looking at Alfie the wrong way, she'd get up and sing 'Respect yourself', to put her friend back on track.

Chic had also got himself back on track. He'd been making plans and invited Lillian down to Seagate Recording Studios so he could outline them to her in the privacy of a sound booth. His intention was to move back to Aberdeen and set up a karaoke show. It was obvious that he wanted Lillian to go with him and he wooed her with the Fredrick Knight number, 'I've been lonely for so long', and the Isaac Hayes song, '(if loving you is wrong) I don't want to be right'.

For the first time, Lillian saw the true potential in Chic. He wasn't just a good hump; he was a good hump who was offering her a half-share in a karaoke show.

That night, they resolved their differences and sang 'Starting all over again', while gazing into each other's eyes, and Lillian promised to tell Alfie 'Bye bye baby', the next time she saw him. Which she did.

The weeks came and went, and things started to return to normal. Mary had even noticed Alfie doing 'Hey girl don't bother me', a few times lately. She never let on to Jan, but her and Alfie were getting on better than they had in ages.

It was because they liked doing it together.

Alfie had thrown a surprise party at the last gig for Mary's birthday, and she was overwhelmed by it all. The whole pub sang the Stevie Wonder version of 'Happy Birthday' and tears of true happiness rolled down Mary's cheeks.

The love between Alfie and Mary was still there and they knew it. Most of the regular punters knew it too, but it wasn't until Alfie stepped on stage that they found it out for real. The song he chose was apt. It was by a local band called Danny Wilson and it encapsulated how he felt at that moment. He wanted Mary back, and the only way he knew how, was to sing 'Mary's prayer'.

The crowd loved it. So did Mary. She knew how he felt, and now it was his turn to find out where he stood. She sang 'Just loving you' with a tenderness in her voice that made most people weep, including Jan.

They closed the show with an old favourite. The same old favourite that they would use to open Friday's show in the Whip Inn.

Everybody joined in and sang, 'Ain't nothing like the real thing', and they meant it.

JOCK TAMSON'S LEGACY

CHAPTER 2

ELLA'S DILEMMA

They were in a taxicab driving east along the Gardiner Expressway en route to their hotel when Ella first became aware of the biting itch that was eating away at the back of her left knee. Battling with herself to ignore the irritation, Ella stared out of the window at the huge expanse of water to the south side of the expressway in search of a distraction. She was missing home already.

Betsy recognised her friend's pained expression.
"Cheer up Ella, it might never happen! What do you say aboot the three o' us havin' wirselz a wee boat trip later in the week? Could be bra!"
"Mmm." Answered Ella, quietly dubious.

Ruth was sitting up front next to the driver, eagerly ogling everything they drove past. A boat trip sounded nice to her. As usual, Ruth showed her true colours when she asked the cab driver which ocean they were driving past.

The Lebanese driver had lived in Toronto long enough to have reached the conclusion that elderly westerners were much the same as elderly Arabs, and that this elderly westerner called Ruth sitting next to him reminded him of his own mother back in Beirut who, on his last visit home, had commented on how beautiful the setting sun was over the ocean when it was really the Mediterranean Sea. Dimitri loved his mother enough to possess a growing fondness for old people whom he deemed 'touched'.

With an abundance of tact and a few tourist brochures which he conveniently kept in the glove compartment, Dimitri explained all about Lake Ontario, boat trips, jet-ski hire, and a "Sheet-load of alternative activities which are a must for senior citizens".

It was to be the holiday of a lifetime. The woman from Asda's head office had said so when she'd phoned Ruth to tell her the good news about winning a holiday for two in the beautiful city of Toronto. Ruth just burst with excitement. She'd always fancied the idea of going to a romantic place like Italy and had promptly told the woman from Asda so. She was only slightly disappointed when she was informed that Toronto was actually in Canada. Funny, Ruth had always thought it was just around the corner from Palermo or someplace like that. The woman from Asda put

Ruth straight. She also put her straight about the Algarve not being in Canada either. Not that too much of that had sunk in. Ruth was so excited about winning that the woman from Asda could've told her anything and she would've swallowed it.

Ruth saw the world in a wonderfully obvious light. A light which, at that moment, began to flicker. A light that conjured up feasible possibilities of what the world was about and what it contained. Her imagination was sharply vivid, especially at times like this. She had to have a vivid imagination, the last time that Ruth went on holiday was during the raspberry-picking season in Blairgowrie, and even then she was only two years old at the time.

Although the holiday was originally for two adults, Ruth, her sister Betsy and their inseparable friend Ella had all chipped in the extra money to make the holiday for two into a holiday for three. There was no possibility of any of them not sharing in the win. Good fortune was a thing to share as far as they were concerned. Conversely, so was bad fortune.

Ella gave the back of her knee a single scratch as she climbed out of the taxi in front of their destination. She knew it was a mistake. She silently swore to herself and a voice inside her head told her that she was as well to have scratched her arse, for all the good it would've done.

"Welcome to the Royal York Hotel ladies!" proclaimed a nearby voice, which reminded Ruth of a John Wayne film, and an army of bellhops with an average age of fifty-six descended on the car, their tip estimations experiencing a downward trend with each advancing step.

The matching shell-suits that Ruth bought in a sale at *What Every Cheapskate Wants* were a dead give-away. They had 'Bargain-Basement' written all over them. Well, not exactly all over them, just down the seams of the trousers, but it was all just too much for one elderly bellhop and he had to be escorted from the scene by the hotel's resident psychotherapist.

After a strained conversation in broken English with a 'Barbie' look-alike at the reception desk, they were eventually escorted to their room – a three-bed affair overlooking a massive railway station with a twinkling marina beyond.

Ruth opened the door to the en-suite washroom and couldn't believe her eyes.

"Come and see this!" she said. "There's twa lavvies in the lavvy! Ain o' them must be fir men jist, cuz there's nay sait!"

Betsy stretched out on a single bed, her head on her handbag and her feet on the suitcase containing their various assortments of pills, ointments, sprays, linctus's, and other precautionary medicines.

"Well, that'll be handy if twa o' us need ti go at the same time!" said Betsy, matter-of-factly.

Ruth was truly astonished.

"What, even if ain o' us are needin' a joby? What kind o' place have they put us in? I've never seen the likes! I'd maybe have understood it if we'd wun a holiday in blimmin' Benidorm, or some other poor wee oot-the-way place in South America whar folk have ti share a lavvy! That blimmin lassie fay Asda telt me that Canada wiz a posh place an' a'! Yi canna trust nay bugger nowadays. Still, I suppose it's better than nay lavvy at a', judgin' by the height o' that sink."

Betsy sensed her sister's moan coming on and was determined not to be drawn in. She was having too much of a good time and was not in the mood for a gripe. She rolled over on to her belly. The bed she'd picked was as comfy as she'd expected, although she would've liked a room to herself. Just in case. Unperturbed by her sister's ranting, Betsy twiddled about with the knobs on the bedside radio and the sounds of Strangers in the night began to flood the room. She joined in with the melody.

"La-de-da-de-da, de-da-de-da-da…"

Ella hung the last remaining frock in the wardrobe and slid the door shut. Although her left knee was giving her gyp, she was determined to hide it from the others for as long as possible.

Joining in with Betsy's la-de-dahing, Ella waltzed around the room before collapsing on her bed in a fit of laughter. Angina or not, buggered-up knee or not, she was going to enjoy this holiday come hell or high water. Starting now. Sod it. The last holiday that she had was when her and Jim went to Eastbourne, and she broke her hip when she tripped over a toffee apple on the pier. It wasn't exactly a happy holiday for Ella, but Jim seemed to enjoy it. God rest his soul. Yeah, Ella would enjoy this holiday fine, contrary to what her left knee was telling her.

This holiday included a host of daily activities to choose from. The three of them liked the idea of the horse-drawn carriage through the bustling metropolis, the shopping excursion to the Eaton Centre, and the day trip to Niagara Falls. The rest, they weren't sure of. They decided to choose one more each.

"What do you think 'The Daughters of Scotland lunch' wid be like?" asked Ruth, her taste buds drowning at the thought of a steaming hot bowl of stovies, or a plate of boiled tatties and potted hoch swimming in melted marg. Or better still, butter.

Betsy was too captivated by the neatly packaged bum of the young man serving behind the hotel bar to have heard her sister properly, but she grunted an agreement anyway.

Ella was more in tune with Ruth. She was missing the creature comforts of home and fancied a decent bowl of soup.

"Sounds good to me Ruthie!" chirps Ella, trying her level best not to give the game away by sounding over eager. "I'd like to go up that C.N. Tower and take some fotayz. That brochure I was readin' this mornin' said it's a hundred an' forty odd flairz tall!"

One hundred and forty odd floors were a tall order for Ruth to imagine. She'd once been up to twelve to deliver some of Betsy's Avon stuff to a woman who lived in the Derby Street multies and the view of the Sidlaw hills from the woman's living room window left a beautifully vivid picture in Ruth's mind.

"That's aboot ten Derby Street multies piled on tap o' each other! That'll be great!" said Ruth, hoping for another glimpse of her beloved hills. "Do you fancy it, Betsy?"

"No' half." smiled Betsy, as the bartender came towards them.

"Can I get you ladies anything?" he said with a welcoming smile designed by his orthodontist to show off his pearly-white caps the way god intended them to be shown off.

Betsy could've done with a fresh pair of knickers but ordered a rum and pep instead. Ella, apart from having a knee which was a pain in the arse, followed suit and had a pint of export, and Ruth, disappointed with the prawn cocktail she'd drunk earlier, opted for a cup of tea this round.

She wasn't feeling too well, Ruth confessed to the bartender, hoping not to have hurt his feelings by ordering a cup of tea in such a posh bar.

The week's itinerary was fixed. The C.N. Tower, the Horse-Drawn Carriage, Niagara Falls, the Daughters of Scotland lunch, the shopping trip, and a day for wandering around doing bugger all in particular but exploring. It was a schedule they all agreed on. Today, they were going to do bugger all in particular and explore.

Ella took an umbrella with her in case it rained, Ruth took a City Centre map in case they got lost, and Betsy took a spare pair of knickers in case they went into any more bars.

Navigating their way through the labyrinth of Toronto's underground streets seemed a good idea at first but after seven hours it became a nightmare. Their thick Dundonian accents sounded like some strange Germanic language with a handful of spittle thrown in to the Canadians. Their hapless pleas to be shown how to get back outside and into the open-air streets, more often than not ended up with them being shown to the nearest ladies' subterranean washroom. They were at their wits end.

To top things, Betsy took a nosebleed. It was just as well they were in yet another lavvy at the time or she would've been forced to use her spare knickers as a hanky in front of everybody. "Ella, tak that bap aff her, for Christ sake!" blurted Betsy through a handful of toilet paper. "Day offence Ruth but yir doh exactly girl scout baterial wi' that bap."

Ruth was glad to hand the map over. She was beginning to wish she'd brought an umbrella like Ella.

Ella just wished that Ruth had taken the Toronto street map from the hotel instead of the Dundee street map.

"This is hopeless! I think that the best way oot o' here is ti try and find somebody that's no' Canadian and ask them!"

A toilet flushed and a woman stepped from one of the cubicles. Betsy, Ella and Ruth were all thinking the same thing. Was she, or wasn't she? They silently watched the woman as she washed and dried her hands. Then they blurted it all out.

Turns out they were all wrong. She wasn't a she at all. She was a he. And the best bit about it was that his father originally came from Falkirk and he was able to understand every word they said. He was their knight in shining sequins.

Three minutes later they stepped out into a real street at last and were glad to breathe real outside air again, even if it was heavily laced with a cocktail of pollutants which gave the city a purple hue on hot sunny days such as this.

They were saved. And Ruth's narrow view of the world had been widened once more. She vowed to herself never again to take a map when she could take an umbrella instead.

Worn out by a day's exploring and a hefty three-course supper, Ruth and Ella looked like they would fall asleep in the hotel restaurant. They were showing their age. Ella was also showing a bra strap and an ever-increasing compulsion to eject her false teeth into a jar of cleanser.

Betsy watched her companions and smiled. What a day. She hoped that the lifts would be working all right in the C.N. Tower the following morning. She'd take some toilet paper with her in case her nose gave out again.

The elevator sped up the tower at thirty-five miles per hour, and the satin knickers with the dodgy elastic that Betsy was wearing over her tights hit the floor at roughly the same speed. Luckily, Betsy was standing at the back of the elevator and the dozen, or so other tourists were looking out of the glass panels at the awesome cityscape below. Glad of the tap-dancing class she'd gone to the other week, she stepped out of her satin knicks like Ginger Rodgers, dropped her shell-suit jacket over the offending flimsies and scooped up the lot like a pensioner at a jumble sale. That was when she noticed it. The very moment that her eyes caught sight of Ella's knee and the scratch marks that adorned it, her head inadvertently turned away to face the opposite direction. Denial was useless. It was there; she saw it with her own eyes. Trouble lay ahead and she knew it. She had to say something about it to Ella and at the same time keep quiet about it in front of Ruth. She'd wait until the moment was right.

Ruth was disappointed at not being able to see her beloved Sidlaw Hills from the Sky-Bubble's observation deck, which was perched one hundred and forty-three floors higher than her bottom-left tenement flat in Morgan Street, but she was quite content to be in awe of the panoramic views over Lake Ontario and of the sprawling city. She was reshaping her view of the world. Oceans like Lake Ontario are too big to build bridges over, that's why everybody lives on this side of the water. Buildings are higher here because the streets are wider. People that live here speak with an American accent because of the amount of TV channels they have.

Ruth wiped a slaver from her chin and calculated the enormity of it all. It took two or three attempts at mime before her brain finally allowed her mouth to tell Betsy and Ella her thoughts.

"I'm hungry wi' a' this height!" said Ruth, "What do yiz say aboot a plate o' tatties an' cabbage at the Daughters of Scotland lunch? A' this global-trottin' is makin' me mad wi' the malnutritions!"

It was a good idea. Betsy was glad of the thought of getting out of the confines of the Sky Bubble so she can get a chance to have a quiet word with Ella, and Ella was glad of the thought of being able to hide her left leg under a table and have a good scratch without causing undue attention.

Ella's knee is an early warning system. A curse. A plague. She's called it many things. None of them accurate enough to convey the implications of her knee's actions. Most people's knees suffer minor ailments like sprains, strains, scabs and occasionally boils, with extreme cases going perhaps as far as a cartilage operation or two. Ella's knee belongs in another dimension. She'd went to see her doctor about it, just the once. Never again. So much for science. All he said was that it was an allergic reaction and gave her a tube of cream. The cream was useless for the itching or the swelling, but it worked wonders for Jim's athlete's foot, which was just as well since it was him that paid for the prescription.

Ella's knee is a supernatural version of the pony express, except that it only brings bad news. Sometimes tragic news. And this time, Ella felt tragic.

By the time they got back to their room, it was almost seven in the evening. It had been a very long day. Betsy and Ella had agreed to wait until they were in the hotel before they broke the news to Ruth. They'd also decided to be anorexic with the truth to avoid setting off Ruth's irritable-bowel syndrome with all the worry.

They all knew that when Ella's knee showed up, trouble wasn't far behind. Somebody close to Ella was going to have a serious case of the misfortunes and if Ruth thought for a minute that it could be her, she would probably wail the hotel down.

The dilemma facing Ella was the identity of the friend or relative who was in imminent danger of pushing up the daisies in the next couple of days.

"I've a feeling it could be somebody at home. Angela maybe... or Steven... or maybe Cousin Annie, she was no' well before wi come awa', it could be her!" whispered Ella, so's Ruth wouldn't hear from the bathroom.

"Okay," said Betsy, "If you think that it's somebody back in Dundee, then you'd better get yirself back there an' find oot wha it is."

Three hours later, Ella walked through the check-in gate at Lester B. Pearson International Airport. She waved her farewells to her best friends, blew them a kiss, and then headed off down a passageway behind a bedraggled young man with a bow-legged gait and a power-dressing woman who looked like she knew where she was going. Ella began to cry.

ELLA'S DILEMMA

Ruth's mouth slavered at the thought of breakfast. She could almost smell the jam through the high-octane fumes, as she walked with Betsy from the airport terminal to a nearby taxi rank. "Ella's got ti be the best pal in the world," said Ruth proudly. "Goin' a' the way haim to Dundee for rolls at this time o' night, just so's we can have a decent breakfast in the mornin'. She's a gem right enough!"
Being worldly-wise was never Ruth's strong point.

JOCK TAMSON'S LEGACY

CHAPTER 3

GREEN

Flipper had to get to the toilet. He didn't like the idea of being sick into the white paper bag that had been provided by the airline. He needed privacy to puke. Thank goodness he didn't have far to walk. Once he was past the old woman with the dicky leg sitting next to him it was only a matter of eight or nine steps, and he'd be in there. His backside clenched at the thought of it, and a ripple of acidic coffee hit the back of his throat as a counteraction.

He needed to go, and he went for it as fast as he could. He jostled past the woman sitting next to him, over some empty seats in the middle row, down the aisle on the other side of the plane, and into trap one.

He'd no sooner bolted the door when the first wave struck. The wash-hand-basin that he was aiming at was as big as a twin-size soap dish, and it deflected the contents of Flipper's stomach back out of the bowl and on to his T-shirt. He didn't care. He was beyond it.

Sweat gushed out of every pore of Flipper's body, and his knees

33

began to buckle and writhe in all directions. He sat down on the toilet seat before he fell down.

He looked at himself in the mirror. It was the first time he'd seen his reflection in three days, and he hardly recognised himself. He was nineteen years old going on fifty by the look of things. After all he'd been through in the past few days, it was hardly a surprise.

Jamaica had been a dream destination of Flipper's ever since he started smoking grass at the age of fourteen. It was the place where it was all happening in a rub-a-dub stylee, and Flipper wanted it. The Bob Marley Museum, Peter Tosh's memorial, Yardies, Rasta's, Reggie music, Ganja; Flipper craved it all.

All the other dealers who Flipper knew were either going to Amsterdam or Spain for their blow, and the punters were growing tired of the glut of Moroccan hashish in the city. People needed a change and Flipper reckoned that he was the one to give it to them.

The offer came out of the blue. Flipper was in the middle of weighing out James's monthly ounce of hash at the time and immediately said, "Too flippin' right!" to the proposition.

James was a regular customer of Flipper's for about a year and a half, and despite the fact that James was a fat middle-class punter in his late forties, Flipper liked him and his cash fine. He liked the guy even more now that he was offering him a chance to fly to the Caribbean and back for less than two hundred greenbacks.

James was the kind of man who seemed to know everybody and have a finger in each of their pies. He never got around to marriage or any of that sort of stuff. He never had the time. He wasn't interested. He was too busy sticking his fingers into places where most folk wouldn't dare. Lately, James had stuck it to the Head of Air Canada's Customer Complaints department and somehow managed to wangle two round-trip tickets to Jamaica for less than the price of a single fare.

Flipper didn't care about the details, he just saw it as an opportunity to broaden his reputation from being a small-time dealer on his home patch in Lochee, to being an international player with a string of Yardie contacts to brag on about.

He had just over four grand in his stash. Plenty.

He contemplated how uncomfortable his bum pocket would be on the way home and winced at the thought. Weighing-up the risk factor, he decided to go for flippin' gold.

The taxi ride from Montego Bay to Treasure Beach was a real eye-opener for Flipper. He'd never known poverty on such a scale as this before and wasn't quite sure of what he was seeing. His eyes homed in on a couple of ragged-arsed kids who were sharpening their machetes on stones at the side of the road and was thankful that he'd been born and raised in Dundee in Scotland, rather than the Dundee that they were driving through at that moment. The names might be the same, but that was where the similarity ended. Back home, people didn't live in rickety shacks on stilts with outside kitchens and ditches for lavvies. And bairns didn't play with knives that were too heavy to lift.

James had been to Jamaica a few times before and knew the score. It was the kind of place that you either loved or hated. James loved it. He felt liberated on this paradise island and hoped that Flipper would grow to feel the same way.

James had booked them into Jake's Place in Treasure Beach. It would be a nice, easy introduction to Jamaica for Flipper. There was no hassle in Treasure Beach to speak of, and it was a safe enough place to go wandering off on your own, if you liked that sort of thing.

It was after nightfall by the time they reached Jake's, and a large pack of dogs, two goats, and a young white guy with a Jamaican accent greeted the taxi.

GREEN

"Wellcam to Jake's Place. Me name iss Rah-bin; I am de proprietor of de cahmplex eer. Eef dare iss anyting special dat you require, you come aks me, okay!" spouted Robin with a beaming smile.

Flipper nearly asked for a half-ounce there and then, but he suspected that Robin was probably talking about extra blankets and towels and things, so he just kept quiet. Anyhow, he was knackered with all the travelling, and the only things he wanted at this stage were some decent grub and a soft bed.

Two hours later he had both.

Flipper woke the next morning and never had a clue where he was. The daft net-curtain that he was wrapped in never helped matters either. It took a full sixty seconds before he realised that he was in Jamaica and that the net-curtain was actually a mosquito net.

He couldn't wait to get out and explore. He was up, showered, dressed, and out the door within ten minutes.

James was down at the pool, paddling in the shallow end. He couldn't swim. He'd never found the time to learn, but that was of no consequence to James. You don't need to be able to swim to ogle half-naked people as they sunned themselves. And that was just what he was in the middle of doing when Flipper showed up and spoiled things.

"Hey James…! Flippin' roastin' or what, eh?" shouted Flipper from the other end of the pool. "Too flippin' hot fir me! I'm awa' ti hit some shade an' git ma breakfast afore I flippin' melt!

James was well embarrassed by Flipper's declaration. He took a deep breath and submerged himself in two feet of water to cool off.

Of course, there was no need for James to feel embarrassed. A lot of people might've heard Flipper shouting, but not one of them understood a word of it. Most of the other tourists about the place were Americans and they were loud in their own right. James thought long and hard about this. Long enough and hard enough to almost drown in two feet of water on his first day in paradise, and if it hadn't been for the quick reactions of a group of local kids swimming nearby, he probably would've drowned.

That first evening, Flipper and James went to the 'Beachcomber Night-club & Bar', a few miles east of Jake's. Flipper was hell-bent on sniffing out the Ganja and James was hell-bent on sniffing out sex.

NO GUNS, NO SHOOTINGS, NO KNIVES, NO GANGA SMOKING, NO KILLING, NO STABBINGS, NO FIGHTING, NO MACHETES, NO PIMPS, NO PROSTIUTES, AND NO LOVEMAKING ON THE PREMISES. By Order of the Management.

The club rules were quite specific. And frequently broken.

James had been in the club before and knew exactly what rule

he was hoping to break. He'd been mentally rehearsing this scenario for weeks. He slicked back his greying hair, sucked in his wobbly belly and headed for the nearest darkened corner.
Flipper got the first round in. A rum punch for James and a bottle of Red Stripe for himself. All Flipper was really interested in was testing out the local weed, and the barman obliged by offering Flipper a ready-rolled spliff of 'Fresh urb', for ten U.S. dollars.

"Some flippin third world country this is!" complained Flipper as he set the drinks down on the table. "You'll never believe what I've just forked oot fir a joint!"
James pulled a brown paper bag the size of an orange from his jacket pocket and placed it on the table.
Flipper was gob smacked when he saw what was inside.
"You should've mentioned that you wanted a smoke! I bought this when I went out for a walk this morning. It only cost me five dollars… do you want some?"
Flipper wanted to kick himself. He wanted to kick the barman too, but he was twice the size of Flipper and probably had a load of mates. He sparked-up his ten-dollar spliff, glugged down half his bottle of beer and sank back into his wicker-basket chair like it was a deep toggle duvet. Flipper was shit-faced almost instantly. That was the last thing he remembered.

Flipper was still shit-faced when he woke. He felt a draught on his legs and thought he must've left the door open when he came in last night. He groped around, hoping to find at least his net curtain and all he found was sand.

Sand? What was sand doing in his flippin' bed?

Flipper opened his eyes and reality hit home. He was lying on a beach surrounded by a group of local children. He'd lost his shoes, he'd lost his Levi 501's, and he lost his sanity when he discovered a slimy, rubbery thing was hanging out of his arse.

By the time Flipper reached Jake's Place he was already a certifiable case under Jamaican law. If he had found James, he probably would've killed him there and then, the sleazebag. Now he knew what the bastard meant when he was going on about sticking his fingers into people's pies, the conniving old bent-shot. Flipper resolved to wait until he was back in Dundee before he'd kill him. Yeah, that's what he'd do.

Flipper grabbed his rucksack and headed North on foot. He was determined to find some Rasta's and do some business before he reached Montego Bay. That was his plan.

It was a plan of a crazy person.

It took Flipper a day and a half to reach Dundee He'd travelled only twenty miles to get to the tiny hamlet, but it felt like a thousand miles to Flipper. He'd been up and down that many steep jungle hills and past so many rickety shacks that he didn't know where he was. He didn't know where his rucksack was either. The last time he'd seen it was just before he fell asleep at a roadside the previous night.

 Flipper didn't recognise the place, but he recognised the machete-wielding, ragged-arsed kids who were rapidly surrounding him and generally giving him grief. He growled at them like a wild animal and to his surprise, they scattered like frightened children.
 It was the first time that the children had seen a white man in the flesh and some of the younger ones hoped that it would be their last. The experience had been terrifying for them.
 It had also been terrifying for Flipper. He was down to his last fifty dollars and didn't fancy losing it to a bunch of kids. He'd already lost his rucksack and the four grand it contained, along with all his belongings. The only things he had left in his possession were his plane ticket, which was safely tucked away in his boot, fifty U.S. dollars, which was safely tucked away under his balls, and a determination to get to Montego Bay airport, catch a five-hour flight to Canada and then another eight-hour flight back to Scotland, and home. The only other things he had in his possession were a crippling pain in his backside and a sickening pain in the pit of his stomach.

 Flipper cleaned himself up. He'd been in the toilet for nearly an hour and an air hostess was hassling him to see if he was alright. He felt a bit better now. He almost looked a bit better too. The thought of being back home in just a few hours lifted his spirits. He'd be more than content to baby-sit with his bonny lass Suzi tonight and fall asleep in her arms as they watch some daft video.

Oh bliss.

CHAPTER 4

THE MEDDLER

He was hoping to be a local councillor. First a lay minister, then a support teacher, then a youth training worker, now a councillor. He just liked the idea of bossing people around or patronising them without them noticing. In short, Hugo Edderington is a man who loves nothing more than fiddling around with people's lives. He's a man with a mission, and his mission is to meddle and manipulate.

Hugo was the youngest son of Sir Edmund Edderington, retired Chief Constable of Wiltshire Police Force, and Grand Master of his local Lodge. Sir Edmund was a bully. A real bully. He bullied for bullying's sake, because it was in his nature and he loved it. He bullied his eldest son, Charles, into the Legal profession, he bullied daughters Margot and Caroline into becoming doctors, he bullied his second son, Ashton into politics, and he attempted to bully Hugo into the God profession. Sir Edmund had aspirations of continuing to bully the public into his way of doing things, through the high-profile positions held by his offspring. And if the public wouldn't play ball, then he would bully his contacts in the Police Force into bullying them for him.

One way or another, Sir Edmund always got his way. He ensured this by keeping a damaging dossier on everybody he'd ever had contact with since his school days. It was something that he had learned at public school from his old Headmaster, Crammond McKenzie, back in the bad old days at Wellington School for Boys.

Crammond McKenzie was the one who twisted and shaped the young Edmund into the bastard that he eventually became. He was a patriotic Scot who was hell-bent on avenging his homeland by inflicting as much pain and torment as possible on the sons of the English establishment. He carried a chip on his shoulder the size of the Great Glen and would think nothing of dangling an eight-year-old boy out of a top storey window in the middle of the night, just to drive that point home. Crammond McKenzie was King of the bullies, and if anybody were to contradict that fact, he would make their lives a living hell for the ten-year duration of their schooling.

THE MEDDLER

The young Edmund Edderington had grown up with aspirations of becoming an accomplished bully so that he could take out his revenge on that old bastard McKenzie and the rest of his bleating countrymen. Sir Edmund, however, became so bogged down with bullying people on his own doorstep that he never did find the time for any long-distance bullying. It was something he'd always regretted.

Hugo had aspirations of becoming a local Councillor. If his father were still alive, he'd be proud of him for sure. Bullying the Scots had always been just a dream for Sir Edmund, but for Hugo it was a reality. He'd been living on the outskirts of Dundee for almost six years and managed to manipulate his way onto fourteen separate Committees, three of which he was Chairman of, and more importantly, eight of which he was secretary and treasurer. Hugo didn't just like meddling with people, he liked meddling with their money too. As a local Councillor, he could meddle with millions.

Hugo's real skill lay in his command of the English language, and of its delivery. His smooth upper-middle-class voice combined with an aloof body language helped him win friends in many places, including the Council Chambers in downtown Dundee. Hence the £200,000 grant aid injection into his Youth Training Project for youngsters from under-privileged backgrounds.

JOCK TAMSON'S LEGACY

The idea behind the project was an old one. It was a big idea that was making a small amount of people very large amounts of cash, by manipulating the loopholes in policies created by idiotic politicians like Hugo's brother, Ashton. Policies which had been legally endorsed by people like his eldest brother Charles. Policies that had the backing of Hugo's breed of people. Policies that were designed to get unemployed people off the streets and turned into useful members of society.

They were useful all right. Very useful indeed. And they were caught in the legal trappings of their unemployable predicament.

Hugo's Youth Training Project had one simple aim in mind; to milk the gravy train for as long as possible, while at the same time supplying favoured business associates with an endless supply of free labour. It was a winning formula which Hugo had been indulging in for the past three years. It was a formula that now required some extra attention, and in Hugo's opinion, that could only be done from within the corridors of the local power base.

Hugo was constantly surrounded by voices. It began in his childhood after his mother had died. They were heavenly voices to a young child. Voices that came to him in the middle of the night and made him think of God. Voices that filled his head with so much bombastic rhetoric it was no great wonder Hugo's life became one big mission.

The voices originally came from a single source. Sir Edmund. He subliminally steered his youngest son towards life in the church, and his method was to bully Hugo's dreams.

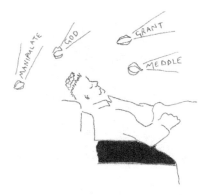

The problem was, the older Hugo got, the more voices he added himself. And if he were to write down a name for each of the voices that haunted his adult life, he'd need a double helping of Andrex lavvy rolls to fit them all on.

The voices that surrounded Hugo first thing in the morning were as alien to him as Punjabi spoken with a Portuguese accent. Young under-privileged people in Dundee certainly had a way with words, but their way remained a mystery to Hugo.

The young folk were quick to recognise that, and frequently took the piss. They may have been under-privileged as far as Hugo was concerned, but they weren't daft. They saw Hugo for what he was. An interfering shitebag.

Friday mornings were the worst, and this Friday was no different. Hugo sat in his office savouring a strong cup of filtered coffee and contemplating the day ahead, when his door crashed open and six-foot three inches of angry Dundonian Neanderthal marched in.

"Story wee the dosh fir the bus fares, pal? Are you takin' the pish or whut? Eh'v been forkin' oot mi ain cash a' week an' it's aboot time eh wiz seein' some o' it back, ken whut um sayin yi bam?!" spouted the Neanderthal through clenched teeth.

Hugo didn't have a clue what the Neanderthal was saying. All he was able to gather from the outburst was that the feral human being standing in front of him was angry about something or another, and that copious amounts of saliva had wound their way from the Neanderthal's mouth into Hugo's coffee. Hugo tried the soft approach.

"Do have a seat, mister...?"

"Fuck the sait! Eh wahnt you ti slap a tenner in this fuckin' hand or yull be wearin' that cup o' coffee on yir wiy oot the windee, savvy ya bass?!"

Hugo analysed the facts so far. Neanderthal bursts in and shouts something. He spits in Hugo's coffee. He shouts something else while pointing at Hugo then pointing at the window, and now he was holding out an upturned hand and glaring at Hugo like he was possessed. The Neanderthal wanted something, that much he was able to surmise. What it was that he wanted completely escaped him.

Hugo did what he always did at times like this. He arranged for somebody else to solve the problem for him. He hit the intercom button on his desk.

"Irene, I have a young man in my office who has a bit of a problem and I need you to deal with it urgently."

"Yes Mister Edderington. Just send him through," came a crackly reply.

Hugo smiled.

The Neanderthal's eyebrow muscle clenched and lowered. He wasn't expecting this outcome. The geek was smiling at him when he was supposed to be keechin' his breeks! He was really looking forward to punching Hugo's face twenty different shades of purple, too! Still, it looks like he'll get his tenner, so the day's turning out pretty good after all!

"Problem solved." said Hugo, still smiling.

The Neanderthal suspected that Hugo was a bit of a turd burglar by the smile he was wearing on his coupon, and there was no way he would allow himself to be smiled at like that. First things first, he would get his money. He could fill Hugo in later. He stormed out of the office with a single word.

"Kentfuckinbettiryifuckinshitethebed!"

Hugo was pleased at the way he'd handled the situation.

"And you have a good day too." He replied to the Neanderthal.

Hugo hated Friday mornings. He was never able to finish a cup of coffee in peace. Still, he was having a business lunch today with a very important client and he would be able to relax and take some caffeine then. Thank God!

Thanking God was one of the things Hugo was good at. He was forever thanking God, or at least the voices in his head were. He used to thank God at least a dozen times per hour with his own voice, much to the annoyance of his family and his local clergy and was even prone to outbursts of scripture quoting when the mood took him. Nowadays, he kept his mouth firmly shut. Excommunication from the Church of England had seen to that. He still believed that the Lord helped those who helped themselves, and that it was his sworn duty as a man smitten by the voice of God to get out into the world and help himself to as much of it as possible. He saw himself as one of the meek and was determined to inherit his fair share of the earth once the non-believing general public had been worked to death for their sins. Hugo considered himself one of the pure and frequently cast the first stone, which usually consisted of stabbing someone in the back in a business take-over, or propagating smear campaigns more complex than anything MI5 could come up with. The bigger the shake-up, the more of a blessing Hugo would confer upon himself. After all, he was a sucker for his own preaching, and if the weak weren't so pathetically feeble he wouldn't have to wreak havoc upon them with the might of the Lord's work. His work. And the work of his associates.

Hugo's twelve-month plan was simple. First, he needed to ensure firm support from as many Company Directors as possible. Company Directors who were tightening their belts as a result of cutbacks in Government spending. Company Directors who were having a hard time finding a sympathetic ear in local Government. More importantly, Hugo was looking for Company Directors whose businesses were ripe for an eventual take-over. Next, he would find a constituency which aspired to snobbishness, and concoct a smear campaign that would make the existing constituency politicians out to be nothing short of devil worshippers. Then, he would step forward with a godly plan of playparks and roses for all and win the next election as an Independent Conservative Councillor. Finally, he would bathe in the coffers, which the council would gladly pay out to the business community. The same business community who was benefiting from his divine guidance and control at their executive meetings.

The work that Hugo had in mind for the rest of the day was the Lords' work and there was no doubt about it, according to one of his voices, and meddling in other people's private affairs was the way forward.

Today would be the turn of a couple of businessmen who had three things in common. One, they were rich enough to warrant attention. Two, they were both recently befriended by Hugo, and three, they were both caught on separate occasions by the telephoto lens of a covert photographer while in compromising positions with a local prostitute, a set of handcuffs, and a very large python named Montgomery.

The Lord does indeed work in mysterious ways.

CHAPTER 5

TOMBOYS DON'T COME INTO IT!

She isn't exactly what you would call, a girlie-girlie type of girl, although, most boys who know her have fantasies about being alone with her on a deserted Island or on a mountaintop somewhere. She's a stunner of a good-looker and she doesn't need lipstick, short skirts and long heels to reinforce it. As far as Iona's concerned, the teenagers of her generation can keep themselves trapped inside their crop-tops, their push-up bras and their crumbling relationships with the opposite sex. She'd rather have her skint knees any day of the week!

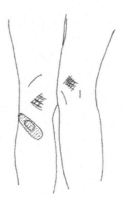

Iona's knees had been torn to shreds on many occasions, so had her elbows, her hands, her ribs, her legs, and her back. Over the years she'd also broken a variety of bones and had lost a tooth, but to her, that was just a combination of bad judgement and bad luck. It was all part of the process. It was something to be expected. It was something that most sixteen-year-old girls couldn't comprehend, let alone expect, but Iona wasn't one of the girlie crowd. She was a girl of exceptional bravery, who was grooming herself for a career as a Hollywood stunt double for all those girly actresses who would shit themselves inside out at the thought of having to fend off the threat of death for real.

Iona's bravery stemmed from her father. He'd helped her bag twenty-three Munros by the time she was nine years old and had introduced her to the joys of abseiling and paragliding when she was only six. He was her father and her mentor, and on a few occasions had been her saviour too.

Iona opened her birthday presents after breakfast. She started with the smallest and worked her way up. Sixteen was an important age and the presents reflected the occasion.

John stood in the doorway with a fresh cup of tea and watched his daughter's meticulous unwrapping ceremony.

"What did yir mum send yi this year?"

"A pair o' earrings and a thirty-pound voucher fir River Island. It's a' right though, I ken she means well! Granny got iz a new slider for my skydiving chute, and uncle Eddie and auntie Dot got iz a beauty o' a pair o' climbin' shoes. This ain um on now's fay Gena and Kev and the rest o' the abseilers up at the club."

"Eh hope it's a handful o' new karabiners, eh'm seek o' mine sproutin' legs an' wanderin' the hills withoot iz!"

"Very funny Pops!" she said with a smile.

She knew that the box in her hands didn't contain any karabiners, it was too light for that sort of thing. It almost felt empty, and at first, she thought it was. Knowing Gena and Kev it's the kind of prank they'd pull. A fart in a box, or something like that.

It turned out to be a kite in the shape of a huge pair of silk bloomers with a note saying, 'We hope you'll find this windsock useful for impressing your paragliding friends!'

Iona was well pleased with the kite. She'd fly it from the top of Cairn Lunkard later this morning to test it out.

It was after ten by the time they reached the car park at Glen Doll. The drive from Dundee took longer than they'd anticipated. John was in dire need of a good stretch and Iona was in dire need of a pee, especially after driving over the cattle grid on the way into the car park.

They'd no sooner stopped when Iona fled the car and headed for the nearest cover. She re-emerged a minute later, glad of the initial relief, and of the fact that she hadn't been wearing her jump suit.

"Whar did you get ti yi skivin' bugger?" jokes John.

"Nay place, I was jist roond the back o' that tree."

"The back o' the tree? So yir a botanist now are yi? How do yi ken it was the back o' the tree? It might've been the side o' the tree, or the front o' the tree, even!" John chips in.

Iona was having none of this nonsense.

"Away an' no be daft, dad! When've yi ever heard o' somebody huvin' a pee at the front o' a tree? Of coors I was at the back! Us weemin ken aboot things like that, yi ken!"

"Oh sorry, so yiz do. It must've slipped my mind wi' a' the heavy unloadin' uv been dayin'!"

"Funny, ha, ha," smirked Iona, "do yi think you'll make it ti the summit the day, or will yi crap oot half-way, like the ald man that yi are!"

The race for the top was on. As always, the banter had seen to that.

The summit of Cairn Lunkard was about two thousand feet higher than the car park. It was situated at the head of the Glen and easily accessible from the mountain track known as Jock's Road. There was no real climb involved and Iona and her dad made the summit in half an hour without breaking sweat.

The view from the top was spectacular. They'd both been there hundreds of times before and they were still gob smacked at the enormity of it all. For Iona and John, it was the only place to be while you're waiting for the wind to rise.

Iona unpacked her silk bloomer kite and launched it on its maiden flight. To her surprise, it took to the air like, well, like a kite! It was a great way to test the air currents and Iona was already wishing she was up there herself.

The normal rate of descent was about three minutes per thousand feet of altitude, but today the warm air was rising faster than usual. They'd decided to try for an extended flight that would take them the length of Glen Doll, and into Glen Clova where they would be able to have a birthday lunch at the hotel. There were always plenty of folk at the hotel who would be willing to give them a lift back to their car, and with today being Iona's birthday, there should be no problem at all.

They soared above the White Water, riding the thermals at four thousand feet and followed the contours of the Glen. It was a clear day, and they could see for miles. The mountain range sprawled northward into infinity where it merged with the streaking clouds and became a blur on the horizon, and Iona and John were in their element.

"Um gled eh emptied oot mi teapot before wi left the car park," Iona shouted over the intercom. "This view's enough ti mak yi want ti wet yirsel!"

"Yir tellin' me! That last cup o' tea that eh had in the hoos is wantin' oot ti play, an' um strugglin' ti keep a check on it!"

"Serves yi right yi ald tea caddy yi! Yi should've went when yi had the chance!" laughs Iona. "You'll be gled wir usin' the Performance gliders the day, an' no' the Standards, eh?"

John was holding his laughter as well as his bladder.

"Let's jist say um gled o' the extra speed, darlin'!"

"Me an' a'!" shouts Iona, and she brakes hard right in search of another thermal. She swoops over the mountain peak, triggering off turbulence from the rocks below to gain some more speed and altitude. She wanted the flight to last longer than her dad's bladder would recommend, but she knew that wouldn't be fair. She knows what it's like to land on a full bladder and she wouldn't want to wish that on anybody, even her dad, although it is fun watching other people's misfortunes.

John wanted to get to the Clova Hotel quickly. He needed to get there before Iona, so he could arrange the surprise with the rest of the local paragliding fraternity. Most of them had already arrived, and he could see the glut of cars at the hotel car park as he descended. He turned the glider and headed into the wind to land. He approached the ground at full speed, pulled hard on both brake cords to flair the glider, causing it to stall and curl the canopy into a gigantic, silken horseshoe, allowing him to step gently on to the grass as easily as stepping off a bus.

"I hope that didna shake yi up too much, mister W.C. in the coo field!" laughs Iona over the radio.

"If you think yi kid day any better, then yid better come ahead! Eh'll have the stretcher waitin' doon here fir yi, dinna you worry, ya cheeky wee bugger yi!" cracks John.

"Hey, less o' the wee, yi ald codger! Jist you get lost oot the way and pay attention ti how it's supposed ti be done!"

"Eh wish eh could darlin, but when yuv got ti go, yuv got ti go, an' right this second eh've got ti be someplace else, if yi ken what eh mean!"

"Roger, wilco and out mister slack bladder sir! Jist you kerry on wi' yir ailment, eh'll be doon in a wee while," shouted Iona, and she drifted off in search of another thermal up-draught.

Iona got the shock of her life when she walked into the Clova Hotel and saw the place packed with her friends. She didn't expect it. She didn't expect them to have all chipped in to get her a birthday present. Most of all, she didn't expect to be the proud owner of a brand-new Competition glider. That was something which had always remained outside her price range but well inside her dreams, and it had been the last thing on her mind prior to tearing open the wrapping. She was stunned. Excited. Humbled. And glad that she could spend the rest of the afternoon riding the thermals with her friends. The day was getting better by the hour.

By the time they got home they were knackered and in dire need of some grub. They were no sooner in the door when the phone rang. They both knew who it would be, and they each wanted the other to answer it.

They flipped a coin for it and Iona lost. She reluctantly picked up the receiver.

"Hi mum." She said quietly.

"Happy birthday sweetie!" Squealed Jill down the line.

"Thanks mum."

"Did you get my gift alright, sweetie?"

"It came this mornin' wi' the furst post." said Iona, as she struggled to free herself from her jacket.

"It's this morning, sweetie, not this mornin'. I do wish you would try and speak more presentably sometimes, darling. Coarse language doesn't suit you, sweetie."

"Yes mum." said Iona, biting her tongue.

"How are the earrings, do you like them?"

TOMBOYS DON'T COME INTO IT!

"Ull have ti get mi ears pierced before eh can try them oot, but um sure they'll suit iz mum, thanks."

"We can always change them, sweetie. How about you coming through to Edinburgh next weekend, and we'll have a look for a pair that you like? We can also have a look round River Island and see if there is anything you'd like to get with your voucher, darling," said Jill, almost patronisingly.

Iona was getting wound up but tried to keep a lid on it.

"Actually mum, it's no' a shop that eh tend ti get stuff oot o'. It's no' my sort o' fashions, if yi ken whut eh mean." said Iona, trying not to sound too hurtful. "Eh was hopin' ti maybe swap the voucher so eh could put the money towards a harness fir mi new glider. If yi dinna mind, that is?"

"When are you going to stop playing all those tomboyish games, sweetie? You're sixteen now, you should be out with your friends, enjoying yourself, meeting some nice young men, doing all the things that sixteen-year-olds do, sweetie."

"Tomboys don't come into it mum! Eh'm no' a tomboy and eh never have been! And as far as being oot wi' mi pals go, you dinna have a clue aboot what eh do or dinna get up ti. You dinna ken any o' meh pals... Christ, yi dinna ken me! River bloomin' Island kid tell yi that!"

Iona couldn't stand the conversation any longer and slammed the phone down. She hated being talked to like that. Nobody else that she knew talked to her like that, and she wasn't putting up with it from an uppity snob who never saw her from one year to the next, even if she was her mother!

Iona needed to get out. She needed to escape.

She grabbed her jacket and her new glider and was out the door in a flash. She was heading for the highest point in the city and there was no stopping her.

"La Hull, here eh come!" she said to herself, as she leapt over the front gate.

Night flights were illegal, and Iona knew it. Night flights over built-up areas were doubly illegal, and Iona knew that too, but she was still raging at the treatment she'd got on the phone, and when she was enraged like that, the only thing that made her feel better was a serious dose of adrenaline, and she knew exactly how to get it. She'd fly from the top of the Law hill, circle the city centre a few times and land in a car park. Preferably, one with hardly any lights.

She was right about one thing. Tomboys definitely don't come into it!

CHAPTER 6

A STREETCAR NAMED ORION

Charlie had a love hate relationship with Friday nights. He wasn't particularly looking forward to it, but he knew it had to be done. It was the hassle more than anything else that he hated. Friday nights brought out the worst in people in Charlie's opinion. For the remainder of the week, most of them were probably nice productive people who wouldn't utter a nasty word to anybody. But this wasn't midweek. This was Friday teatime. The lull before the storm. Goodbye cherubs, hello demons.

Charlie's biggest demon was himself. He was riddled with greed, and he'd known it from an early age. He was a slave to free enterprise who loved the sight of cash in any shape or form. He was a money junkie and a hard-working one at that. A cabbie without a conscience, who had a deep loathing and extensive track record of bummer Friday nights. He hated it, but his preoccupation with paper money and coinage always got the better of him, and a Friday-night cruising he would go... after sifting through the debris of the day shift, that is.

Charlie slipped a five pence piece into his back pocket without as much as a thought as he searched down the back of the rear seats for any more fallen coins. He pulled out a disposable lighter. Empty. He hated folk who disposed of their disposables down the back of his seats, but he loved the folk who were careless with their cash. He checked under the front seats. An empty crisp packet and a ballpoint pen. Still, in Charlie's opinion it's better than finding broken glass or dog shite.

63

JOCK TAMSON'S LEGACY

Friday night for a taxi driver, means singles night in trade talk. It also means the best takings and tips of the week. Friday night is the night when couples young and old opt to travel in separate taxis to rendezvous with their friends, rather than be seen to be going out with their mate (a social activity traditionally reserved for Saturday nights). Lately, Charlie's Friday night takings were as low as his Tuesday afternoons, the exception being Tuesday past, which netted him an extra eighty quid for ferrying three old biddies to Edinburgh airport. Last Friday night he was off the road early because of a bloke who boaked-up his lasagne and vodka all over the dash, the carpet, the seat, the windscreen, and Charlie's leg. The week before that he was in the house by eight o' clock, after a well-to-do woman dogged-up to the nines went and pished her drunken self all over his back seats. This Friday was going to be different; he could feel it in his water.

Charlie'd been a taxi driver for the past eighteen years. He'd started on the very day that his daughter Margaret was born and was so excited about being king of the road that he ended up being nine hours late for the birth. His new-found quest for the elusive couple of quid had taken him to every corner of the city before he managed to find a fare that wanted to go to Ninewells Hospital. Walking into the hospital that day, he'd felt so proud. He was jingling with self-satisfaction at how well he'd reacted to his predatory instincts while cruising the city streets in his Cortina. He'd obviously forgotten that all humans are world champion predators and that his wife was no exception.

In the quiet serenity of the postnatal ward, Wilma gave Charlie such a severe bollocking for being an inconsiderate bastard, that even the nurses were embarrassed. Her predatory instincts were to do the human thing and make the self-indulgent swine pay. After all, where was he when she was in the delivery room being hooked up and sliced open? Halfway to someplace or other hoping for a tip probably, selfish nyaff that he is! She'd make Charlie pay all right. And she started with the eighty-five pounds he had in his wallet, thank you very much.

Eighteen years on, Charlie had well and truly learned his lesson. If he thought for a minute that Wilma was pissed-off at him for something, he'd stash his ten and twenty-pound notes in his sock before going home to face the music, regardless of what tune she was playing.

Charlie gave his windscreen a final buff with a small lump of kleenex, slipped behind the wheel of his Ford Orion and took a slow downhill drive to the rank at the railway station. It was a busy place at tea-time, and he hoped he wouldn't have long to wait for a fare. He pulled up at the back of the rank and counted the taxis in front of him. Only twelve. That was a good sign for Charlie. It meant hanging around for only five or six minutes. He walked up to the front of the rank, to where a small gathering of drivers were standing gassing.

"A' right Boab! Howzit hingin' Geordie, is there a train due or what?"

"There's ain due at forty-three past, ain at forty-eight, a fifty-one and twa due at fifty-six past," blurted Geordie like a pre-recorded telephone message. "You've six meenits yet." he added as an afterthought.

"I see you've still got that bucket o' shite yi call a taxi, Charlie. When are yi gonna dip inta that bankbook o' yours an' get yirself a motor that's no' a death-trap for a change?" Boab pipes in.
"Nothin' up wi' the fordee orions Boab. Better than that tappet-rattler you're scootin' aboot in! Yi must be seek tellin' yir customers it's a time bomb, are yi?" chirps back Charlie.
The slagging banter went on for the duration of the wait.

As far as Charlie was concerned, six minutes can drag out to feel like an hour if you're sitting in the cab doing nothing, but when you're having a dig at somebody it passes in a flash. Charlie flashed a dig at every driver on the rank, every cab, students in general, pensioners, and anybody else who came to mind as he waited the forty-three minutes for his first fare to arrive, and by that time, his earlier optimism had been quelled to a bitter mood.
The fare was a cracker. A young lassie wearing an old woman's overcoat, going to Carnoustie. That perked Charlie right up! A twelve-pounder with the meter off was just what was needed to raise Charlie's expectations of the night ahead.

A STREETCAR NAMED ORION

The usual conversation ensued.
"Been busy today?"
"Just started my shift, you're my first fare."
"Oh."
Quarter of a mile further along the road...
"What kind of car is this?"
"A Ford Orion."
"Oh."
Two more miles of silence, then Charlie took control of the conversation. He considered himself an expert in taking control of conversations. He was cool. He was slick. He was subtle. He wanted to know why a young lassie that should be dressing herself up like Taylor Swift was wearing her granny's overcoat? He applied a little tact.
"What's the story wi' the granny jacket. Like the ald fashioned stuff do yi?"
Her response was slow at first. She'd been teetering on the edge for the best part of the day, but now she blurted it all out between fitful sobs to Charlie, like he was a priest.
Charlie played for the tip every time he had single passengers in the car. This time, his tip play would be sympathy-giver with a touch of jester thrown in for light relief.

He oh'd and ah'd in sympathy as the lassie told him about her day trip to Burntisland, the golden retriever dog on the beach, and how the mangy canine picked up her dress in its slavery mouth and legged it off somewhere while she was enjoying a wee swim in the buff. And if it weren't for the kindness of an old woman lending her an overcoat, she'd probably still be in the water hiding her wrinkly bits. By the time they were driving through Monifieth, Charlie was beginning to regret having struck up the conversation. He'd lost track of what she was saying about half a mile ago and there were still a few miles still to go before he got shot of her. He played the sympathy card a little longer, in the hope of doubling his tip.

What Charlie'd forgotten about, (or never quite heard with all his Ohing and Ahing) was the fact that the lassie had also lost her purse to the mangy mutt on the beach, and that her mum would be paying the fare once they got to Carnoustie.

Her mum was a nice enough woman, full of the apologies for the state of her daughter and of her endless thanks for Charlie driving the lassie home safely.

Charlie knew the sketch. He knew punters well enough to know that the more praise and thanks they gave him, the less of a tip they would give him, and by the amount of verbal coming out of this woman, he resigned himself to only getting the twelve quid.

A STREETCAR NAMED ORION

Fuck it, he should've priced the job at fifteen in the first place.

Charlie was right. No tip. He wouldn't play the sympathy card again tonight. Too risky. He felt like he'd just lost a five-pound note and if this sort of thing were to go on all night, he could end up skint, God forbid.

Charlie accelerated out of Carnoustie like Beelzebub was tickling his sphincter. He sped through a few miles of countryside, and was halfway through Monifieth before he realized he was still doing sixty. He slowed down to thirty-five and scanned the pavements.

Charlie saw the guy coming out of the pub from about two hundred yards away. The guy took two steps forward, one to the side, another forward, and Charlie knew immediately that that was the guy for him. The guy looked respectable enough, and if he spewed-up in the taxi, Charlie would hit him for a sixty-pound cleaning bill no problem.

The guy was able to focus through only one eye at a time and was lucky to have noticed the taxi at all. If it hadn't been for Charlie stopping at the kerb beside him, the guy would've been there all night.

Charlie knew he shouldn't be picking up fares outside the Dundee City boundary and if he was caught picking up fares in Monifieth he'd probably lose his licence. What the hell, they've got to catch him first!

Another half-decent fare. The guy was going to the centre of Dundee to pick up his car from the car park where he'd left it earlier in the day. He slumped into the front seat and was throwing out zeds by the time Charlie got into top gear.

Charlie quickly seized the opportunity and took a long-cut through a few adjacent housing schemes. Well, after all, the guy was drunk, snoring, and incapable of coherent observation, and if Charlie didn't take advantage of a situation such as this, he wouldn't have anything new to tell the lads on the rank, would he?

Fifteen minutes later, he pulled into the West Port car park and cut the engine. The guy was still zonked, and Charlie had to get out, open the passenger door, give the guy a good shakedown and pull him to his feet in order to get paid. Charlie deftly relieved the guy of his last twenty-pound note and left him propped up against a silver BMW with a soft top and steaming warm sick on the bonnet.

"Charlie, Charlie, you're red-hot the night!" He mumbled to himself, as the taxi cruised slowly out of the car park.

The next hour and a half ticked along nicely for Charlie.

A STREETCAR NAMED ORION

The city centre to Lochee; Lochee to the Hilltown; the Hilltown to Douglas; Douglas to the West End; the West End to Broughty Ferry, and now, a belter going from the Ferry, up to Castle Park, then on to the Logie Club in Lochee. Another eight-pounder!

The feeling that Charlie had had in his water at the start of his shift seemed right about tonight being Charlie's night. It was only a quarter to eight and he'd already made nearly sixty quid, he now had a beautiful long-legged teenage lassie in the back seat, and he was beginning to have visions of topping the hundred-pound mark by ten o' clock.

Yeah, tonight was going to be clean-cut. Charlie could feel it in his water.

JOCK TAMSON'S LEGACY

CHAPTER 7

BORDER PATROL

Robbie climbed the trunk of the huge Beech tree with ease. His toes fitted perfectly into the notches that his grandfather had carved into the tree over fifty years ago, and he crept up the trunk like a shadow. He'd done it a thousand times before, just like his forefathers had done, only, this was the first time he'd tried to tackle the tree at twilight. It was easier than he'd anticipated.

The McNicols had been living on the edge of Dundee for over three hundred years and had been living with an insanity problem for almost as long. It began with Robertson McNicol the first, Robbie's namesake. He was the initial crazy. He was the one who started the family tradition of hating the nearby City and its inhabitants.

It was an annoyance more than anything else at the beginning, and old Robertson was sick of it. His land was being trampled to death under the onslaught of people who were crossing the Sidlaw hills from the lands of Airlie and the Vale of Strathmore and were heading to the City in search of their golden dreams. Robertson was sick of it. He was sick of his tatties being robbed, he was sick of his dykes being knocked over from bairns climbing all over them, he was sick of his trees being cut down to be used as firewood for tinkers and their clans. He was sick of it! So, he shot and killed three of them. He blamed it on the City Fathers for enticing a load of ne'er-do-wells to come and work in their mills, and all he was doing anyhow, was trying to keep a lid on the vermin population. His defence fell on deaf ears, and he was swiftly dispatched to meet his maker at the end of a very long rope, which was slung over a heavy-duty limb of a very large Beech tree.

Shooting trespassers and blaming it on the city became a tradition within the McNicol family and was often employed as a rite of passage from boyhood into manhood. Over the generations, eighteen McNicols have followed old Robertson's lead and ended up swinging from very long ropes, three have been shot, one was sent to the gas chamber and four were incarcerated in various institutions.

The Beech tree that Robbie was climbing had been planted at the turn of the 20th century by Hamish McNicol, his Great, Great Grandfather. It had been planted to mark the eastern boundary of their land where it met the estate of Camperdown and was intended as an investment for the future pursuits of his descendants.

Hamish was a pacifist at heart and had no intention of hurting a soul. However, Hamish also understood the fact that not every McNicol thought the same way as he did, and at some time in the future, a descendant of his was going to take a pot-shot at one of the townies. And if they were going to go about taking pot shots at people, they were better off doing it from a good vantage that can overlook the road that flanked the boundary. In planting the tree, Hamish hoped to put an end to the death toll on his ancestral land. His descendants could take the fight outside.

Robbie was taking the fight outside. He was fulfilling his destiny and about to become a man. He knew that once he'd taken up his position in the tree he might have a long wait, so he came prepared. A packet of chewing gum to help him concentrate like they say on the advert, a packet of cheese and onion crisps and a Snickers in case he got hungry.

His only problem was thirst. The inside of Robbie's mouth felt like it had just been hoovered and he'd forgotten to get a can of juice when he was up at the petrol station on the Coupar Angus Road. It was a mistake that he wouldn't repeat. It was the mistake of a boy who was about to become a man. It was the first mistake of the evening, with a good deal more to come.

Back to the petrol station and Robbie reached into the refrigerator and pulled out a can of cola and an orange squash drink. He was contemplating a long, dry wait ahead, so he decided on two drinks. The orange squash for on the way back down the road and the cola for if he got thirsty again while he was up the tree. He closed the fridge door and headed for the counter.

Thirty seconds later he was striding out of the petrol station stone-faced and extremely pissed-off. He'd forgotten that he was wearing his combats and had left his money in his school trousers, back in his bedroom. He felt like a real dickhead.

He dug deep into his pocket and took out a small notepad and pencil. He wrote himself a note to remind himself that the woman who worked in the petrol station was a mouthy Dundonian immigrant and should be shot at his earliest convenience.

If it wasn't for the fact that he'd left his high-powered .22 air-rifle stashed up a tree, he probably would've taken a pop at her right there and then, and as far as Robbie was concerned, she would've deserved it.

Robbie decided to head home and stock up from there instead. His only reservation was that he'd also left his house keys in his school trousers, and he wasn't sure if he'd get in. It was Friday, and his mum and dad were out on the piss somewhere. The house would be empty, and he contemplated taking full advantage of his dad's whisky decanter once he got there.

BORDER PATROL

Robbie slid open the bathroom window and climbed inside, ripping the pocket of his combat jacket in the process. He was devastated. He'd bought the jacket as a special treat for tonight and now it was ruined. He made a mental note to get it stitched-up by his mum before his next patrol.

As Robbie's foot came into contact with the floor, the burglar alarm kicked in. Lights flashed on and off all over the house, and the noise was so intense that Robbie was sure his brain was going to burst.

He punched the code into the alarm control box and the house fell silent although, the residual noise continued to rage inside Robbie's head for a while longer. He needed a drink to calm himself and soothe his eardrums and that was a fact.

He'd never drunk whisky before and wasn't sure how much to pour. He settled on only half-filling the mug and topping up the other half with his mum's homemade raspberry cola. He'd seen his uncle Callum drink it this way, so he knew it was a man's drink, and since he was about to become a man before the evening was over, he felt nothing wrong in indulging in a bit of early practice.

JOCK TAMSON'S LEGACY

Alcoholism was also a tradition with the McNicols. Over the centuries, they were either strung-up or strung-out, and quite often both. Since many of the men folk were in the habit of dying off at an acutely early age, many of the womenfolk took to distilling whisky and selling it to their relatives and friends to make ends meet. It was a tradition that fanned the flames of hatred. A tradition, which was now being enjoyed by a fifteen-year-old boy who had a high-powered air rifle hidden in a beech tree.

Robbie threw back his drink like a child taking a spoonful of horrible medicine. He downed the whole mug in four successive glugs. If it wasn't for the rancid smell of the stuff and the bloody awful taste, he might've enjoyed it a bit more.

He might've been disappointed with the smell and the taste, but he certainly wasn't disappointed with the effect. The fire spread from the pit of his stomach and engulfed his body in seconds. His arms and legs fell victim to impulsive and independent flailing, causing Robbie to collapse onto the kitchen floor, splitting his head open in the process.

Although there was now a two-inch gash in the back of his head, and his vision was starting to go wonky, all Robbie was able to do was summon up what little strength he had left and laugh.

BORDER PATROL

Tonight wasn't turning out strictly according to plan and if anyone knew it, he did. He made a mental note to clean the blood from the kitchen floor before his mum and dad got home. They'd go ballistic and ask loads of questions and stuff if they saw it and he didn't want to get into any trouble, so he'd mop it up after he'd shot his first Dundonian. Yeah, that's what he'd do! He'd come back, clean the floor, top up the decanter with cold tea and act as if nothing had happened. He might even do the dishes if he can find the time.

Finding the time was one thing. Finding the front door key was quite another, so Robbie left the house the same way as he got in in the first place. Only this time he was rather more rat-arsed drunk, and his vision wasn't twenty-twenty any longer, it was more like fifteen-three.

Robbie tumbled out of the bathroom window into a patch of his mother's floral assortments. The view from the flowerbed seemed alien to Robbie but he knew that once the world stopped spinning and twisting and changing colour he'd finally recognise where he actually was.

The spinning and twisting were signs that Robbie didn't recognise. He'd smoked a joint at school once, and never had this reaction. He'd even tried sticking his dad's lighter fuel up his nose but all that did was made him stink of petrol for a couple of weeks. The spinning and twisting was a mystery. Until, that is, the ground beneath him began to churn, like he was on a boat in the middle of the river Tay in a heavy swell.

Spinning + Twisting = ?????

Spinning + Twisting + Churning = Pukesville!!

Robbie barfed a steady stream of whisky and raspberry cola for what seemed like an eternity, and he was glad when the world finally stopped wobbling about out of sync with his guts and started behaving itself again. He had a job to do, and if his eyes would just stop watering, and his mouth would shut off the salt-water supply that was flooding out and clinging to his jacket, he'd get on and do it.

He reached the coal-bunker and hauled himself to his feet. Only three fields to go and he'd be back in position. He hoped that the world would stay still long enough for him to get there without throwing up again.

As Robbie staggered through the barley field, he thought of his grandfather, Rory. He made a mental note to go and visit him in the institution sometime soon.

During the war against Hitler, Rory was lucky enough to secure the position of Corporal in the Home Guard, which was based in nearby Birkhill. He was a popular man, and with the advent of rationing, his family's continual whisky production made him even more popular. Rory was a natural-born trader and had soon amassed an arsenal of weapons and explosives, which he intended to use against the spineless Dundonians who were conscientiously objecting to getting themselves blown to bits in glorious battle and were high-tailing it out of the City and into the hills.

The war came and went, and Rory hadn't come across any spineless Dundonians. He assumed that they were all too scared to leave their homes, so he buried his cache in a variety of strategic sites around the farmhouse. He connected each cache to a central triggering device, that was also buried.

The explosives were in the barley field. Robbie already knew that. Where the triggering device was, was anybody's guess. He'd definitely have to pay a visit to the institution soon, hopefully on a day when his grandfather wasn't too shit-faced on his medication to recognise him.

Robbie reached the Beech tree and slumped against it, giving it a drunken hug. He loved that tree and wasn't scared to show it, especially now that it was dark enough to do it without being seen. He caressed the notches that his grandfather had carved into the trunk and his thoughts turned to the new lassie in his maths class. She had a bum like two hand-grenades in a Tesco carrier bag and Robbie fancied her rotten. He made a mental note to ask her for a shag on Monday morning after assembly. He'd be a man by then and she wouldn't be able to resist his manly charm, would she?

Robbie dragged himself up the tree and recovered his weapon. It was loaded and ready to go. He crawled along a heavy limb overhanging the road and perched himself in his ideal shooting position.

Tonight will be his night of glory. He's following in the footsteps of his ancestors. He's Robertson McNicol the fourth, and he's about to become a fully-fledged icon in his family history. He's about to become a man, and he's determined to do it, even if it takes him the rest of his life.

CHAPTER 8

THE BABYSITTER

That phone voice of hers got right on Lenny's wick. Legacy of the job he supposed. Lenny just wished that she didn't bring it home with her, but she did. Every night. He hated it. Mind you, he hated most things about his wife nowadays, so it's no surprise that he hated that patronisingly dominant tele-sales voice of hers as well.

"The taxi's due to arrive at seven forty-five. I'll give it another ten minutes before I send Leonard out to look for her in the car."

The first thought that entered Lenny's head was, "And that will be right!" The second thought that entered his head was the fantasy of Suzi's long, fit, eighteen-year-old legs sitting next to him in the car. The third thought that entered his head was too much to cope with, especially with his wife in the same room.

Lenny rolled a ciggie to bring himself back to reality. Like father like son, Golden Virginia was a constant semblance of control to be exerted on the mind. Pornographic thoughts and hand-rolling tobacco don't exactly mix, which goes some way in explaining why Lenny chain-smokes roll-ups when his wife's around.

Lenny knows the pattern on nights like this. Nights when they're supposed to be going out together to some do or another. This time its Sadie's anniversary do at the Pan-Loafy Hotel in Monifieth.

Whatever it was that had happened to Lenny's wife had also happened to Sadie. Lenny wasn't sure if it was a woman thing or what. He suspected it was, but then again, he can remember there being two or three lads that were in the same year as him at school being a bit like that. Thinking that they were toffs. Always swanning around, attempting to talk posh like they were everybody else's intellectual and social supremos.

Lenny gave one of them a bleeding nose one time. Douglas Rogers was his name. He deserved it as far as Lenny was concerned, and it was well worth the four whacks of the Deputy Head's belt, so it was. I mean, you can't expect to call somebody a 'placental rejection' and get away with it now, could you? That was Lenny's excuse to the Deputy Head. That's probably why he got four whacks that day instead of the usual two.

Lenny liked Sadie as much as he liked Douglas Rogers and the Deputy Head. He definitely wasn't looking forward to spending an evening in her condescending company, listening to all that guff about her patio, her curtains, her hard-working man who still finds time to traipse around supermarkets and DIY warehouses with her on a Sunday, her two wee dogs, and her bairn's outstanding academic achievements since she was enrolled in the High School down by the Albert Square.

The thing about Lenny's wife was, she always wanted something other than what she already had. She wanted to move out of the scheme where they were both brought up and move into a Betts house in Castle Park, so they did.

Before they'd moved, she'd loved the Betts house. She loved the shape of the house, the colour, the windows, and the garden. The thought of having nice hard-working, professional, middle-class people as neighbours appealed to her sense of status.

Lenny barely got the first carpet tack hammered home when the first change of plan happened. The new carpets cost him an extra four grand and a fortnight off work while his broken finger recovered from the hammer blow. In the eight years since, Lenny had repeatedly lost count of the number of times he'd broken his fingers as a result of his wife's whimsical suggestions. It was his last visit to the casualty department that brought him to his senses. He took the doctor's advice and stopped being such a wimp. Only, in Lenny's case, he took this advice quite literally and applied the basic theory to cover all aspects of his married life.

"I hope you don't think that you're smoking those things tonight!" she thundered at Lenny, as the well-practised smile on her thin lips collapsed into a venomous sneer.

Lenny hadn't even noticed that she'd finished on the phone. Her bark snapped him back to reality.

"Away'n shite!" he replied with an air of dignity.

The pattern was beginning a repeat cycle. It was always like this. Well, ever since Lenny started standing up for himself it was. Ever since the 'New Man' became a 'New Man'.

Lenny decided on a follow-up to speed the proceedings along.

"An' if you think I'm drivin' aboot in the car lookin' fir the baby-sitter, jist cuz you went an' telt her mithir that I would, then yi can jist birl on that!" he said, brandishing his roll-up.

"Why do you always have to start an argument before we go out? Why can't you just be normal like everybody else?"

"Look Iy-reen..!"

"And stop calling me 'Iy-Reen'! Why can't you call me 'Eye-rean' like everyone else does? It is my name, you know!"

"Ever since we moved here it hiz been! A posh hoos rapidly follay'd beh a posh name if yi ask me!" Lenny chirped back to his ever-increasingly distraught wife.

Lenny had wounded her in her Achilles heel. He knew what it was that made her vulnerable. He knew her demons. He'd rummaged around in the cupboard where she kept her skeletons many a time.

THE BABYSITTER

Most folk are proud of their roots, their childhood days, their old school pals. Not so for Irene. At school she was known as 'Iy-reen McBean, the toffee-nosed queen!'. Marrying Lenny to become Mrs Calder and moving from Fintry to Castle Park was part of her plan to shake herself free of what she perceived as a working-class bondage chain, that was mistakenly placed around her neck at birth.

Irene exploded. "You always do this to me! What is it with you? I really do think you should see a Doctor Leonard, you know that! You're mad! Crazy! Flipped! You're definitely in need of some help!"

Lenny expected this. He knew the pattern. Thrust, Parry, Thrust, Parry, Thrust. More often than not, she would begin with a dig at Lenny, which would immediately be deflected, then he would follow through with a strike at one of her impending plans. She would always retaliate by calling Lenny's sanity into question, and in doing, elevating herself to the moral and intellectual high-ground. Lenny used to be a sucker during this stage in the proceedings. There had been times where he actually thought he was going insane. Subtle comments over a long period of time can do amazing things with someone's autosuggestion mechanism and Lenny's was no exception. He actually began to think that he was going off his nut. That was before his autosuggestion kicked up a gear. That was then. Now he knew better. Now he knew the pattern. He felt in control, now that he knew the pattern and his wife didn't, and he'd convinced himself of his sanity once and for all.

Lenny casually reached above the coal-effect gas fire and unhooked the mirror. Calmly, he turned to face his wife.

Irene wondered what he was doing. She looked at her reflection, spotted a stray hair and puffed it back into place.

"What's this in aid of Leonard, scared I'll go and phone the doctor?"

"No Iy-reen, I thought yi might've been confused there between sane and insane. The mirror's to let yi see whut a real case o' the insanities looks like."

Lenny hooked the mirror back on the wall, mildly pleased at his latest thrust.

"You bastard!"

Irene didn't like that at all. She recognised Lenny's line of attack. She'd seen it before and didn't like it then either. He was just a bastard and that was that. There was nothing wrong with her sanity. Was there? No, of course there wasn't! He must be mad to even suggest the possibility of it being her who's in need of a doctor! He must be mad. Mustn't he? Why does he do these things? Because he's crazy. Yeah, that's it.

Lenny decided to shift up another gear.

"That's twin'ay-fehv ti eight. The taxi'll be here in ten meenits. Eh'm awa up ti check on the bairn."

He wanted her to stew in her own thoughts for a while so, as he nipped out the door he thrust once again, this time with a small one, just enough to keep her panicking all the same. He let it slip out like a mild truce. Like he was almost on her side for a moment.

"God knows whut wir gonna day if that baby-sitter dizna show."

And with that, Lenny was out the door and climbing the stairs three at a time.

Irene stood motionless for a moment, contemplating a contingency plan. Lenny's desired affect had been achieved. Her breathing became faster and faster, her lips became thinner and thinner, her teeth clenched tighter and tighter, her compulsion to scream grew stronger and stronger, but she held it well. Well, maybe not.

From upstairs in the bairn's room, Lenny only heard some of it. He heard the "Shite shite shite" and a couple of other not-so-mild swearies, a growl or two, and a variety of assorted bumps, thumps and slams. Lenny allowed himself a little laugh.

"Mad bastard."

This wasn't the first time Lenny had done this, oh no. Lenny liked revenge, so he did. Sometimes the bairn woke up with all the noise. That's when he enjoyed that type of revenge the best. When he could share it.

Wee Victoria might only be eighteen months old, but she'd already picked up the basics. She knew the difference between a loving parent and a crazy parent. She'd heard the description many a time. From both her parents. Sometimes she heard it while she slept. Like now.

"Mad bastard... yi see darlin', she's trehin' ti make oot that it's me who's the crazy in this hoos when a' alang it's that mentul case. Listen ti yir ma thowin' a bairnish tantrum doon there. Shiz fukt-up an' there's nay doot aboot it darlin'."

The loving parent was the one who told her these things. The things about the crazy parent. It never worked the other way round. The crazy parent would never say anything about the loving parent. It was always the loving parent who taught her about the condition known as crazy. Loving parents tell the truth, don't they? They must! They must love their children. They say so. Lots. Victoria knew she was loved. Her mum and her dad had been telling her that ever since she could remember. So, in order for Victoria to be loving, she knew she also had to be crazy. It stands to reason. She'd tried imitating the crazy parent on occasion, but it never really worked. She still had a lot to learn and plenty of time to learn it. She'd been privy to having both parents crazy a few times. But even then, she'd only managed to learn snippets of what crazy parents were doing when they were busy being crazy. The learning curve would usually come to an abrupt end after one of the crazy parents would shout something like, "Di yi want the bairn ti grow up thinkin' shiz got a couple o'

90

mentul cases lookin' eftir ir!" She's got a lot to learn yet though. Still, she's got two loving parents to teach her. And one of them was in the process of teaching her when the doorbell rang and spoilt everything. Victoria didn't mind. She was sleepy and wanted to get back to her dreamy game with the furry thing and the ice-cream.

 Lenny sneaked downstairs like a true predator and perched himself quietly on the bottom stair, listening to the calm in the house. Waiting. Waiting for his moment to strike. He never had to wait long. The first thing he heard was, "A lorra foon.." That was it. That was his cue. The TV was now on full-blast volume and showing an old repeat where Cilla Black was doing her bit.

 Lenny opened the living-room door and meandered in, carrying with him a convincing air of disappointment and boredom.
"Wiz that the taxi?"
Irene kept her eyes firmly fixed on the TV. She was simmering on a low peep and grinding her teeth.
"Are we goin' oot or what?" Lenny couldn't resist it. He liked having a follow-up.
 Irene tilted her head slightly towards him. Not enough to meet face-to-face though. Her face was tripping her.
"What do you think?"
 Lenny was expecting exactly this, so his reply might be

considered as 'one that had been prepared earlier'.

"Correct me if um rang, but eh thought that we wir goin' oot!"

She took that thrust and allowed herself to be wracked in pain by it. She really had wanted to go. But she knew all along that she wouldn't be going.

"Well, eh'm biydin' in!" she snapped.

Success. He'd cracked it. He knew that when he heard Irene's real voice coming through the polished cracks, he was almost home. He thrust once more. Hard and loud this time.

"Eh nyoo it, eh nyoo it...! Eh dinna ken how eh waste mi time even gittin' misel' ready! Eh nyoo this wid happen'! Yi day this every single time! Well, up you! Eh'm no bydin in wi' you wi' a face like that!"

"Well how di yi no' jist fuck off and git oot then!" she screamed in her native tongue.

Lenny managed to get the last word in.

"Eh wehll, eh fukin' wull then!"

He slammed the living room door behind him, snatched his coat from the hook beside the front door and stormed his way down the path and along the street. As soon as he was out of sight of the house, he relaxed a bit. He pulled an old polo mint from his coat pocket and gave it a dusting down. It didn't look that old. He chucked it in his mouth. He spotted the taxi at the end of the street. The headlamps were off. As he got close, the engine came to life and the headlamps beamed on. Lenny spat out his polo, opened the back door of the cab and climbed in.

Suzi's long, fit, eighteen-year-old legs pressed hard against his, and fantasy, yet again, became reality.

As soon as Irene heard the clang of the gate she was off her backside and on the phone.

"Mister Rogers please." She waited. "Douglas, it worked! I'll put the electric blanket on. You can bring the baby oil this time!"

THE BABYSITTER

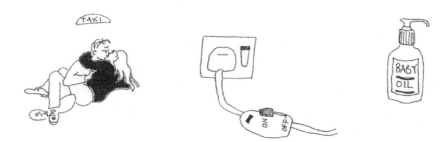

JOCK TAMSON'S LEGACY

CHAPTER 9

THE ROAD AND THE MILES

Jackie opened his eyes as best he could. He couldn't recognize his surroundings at first, but it didn't take very long for the penny to drop. He was sitting in his car, that much he was able to figure out. How he got there was anybody's guess, and where he was parked was a complete mystery to him.

Jackie's senses had been dulled by the vast amount of alcohol that was coursing through his veins, and one by one they slowly returned, revealing the world in which he found himself.

His sense of smell was next to awaken, and his nose filled with an acidic stench that made him want to retch. He caught the unmistakable whiff of puke, and his mind registered it almost immediately.

His taste buds went straight to work as his tongue probed the inside of his mouth. He tasted coconut, and his brain reminded him of the afternoon he spent in the pub with Hugo Edderington, and of the bottle of Malibu he downed while he was there.

He couldn't figure it out. His nose and his mouth were sending him contradictory messages. He probed his mouth once more, just to be on the safe side. Nope, definitely no taste of puke there. He just couldn't figure it out! Mind you, he was still held fast in a state of drunken oblivion, and there wasn't that much he was able to figure out in general anyway.

He reached into the glove compartment in search of a buckshee packet of smokes. There were none. He tried his jacket pocket, and immediately, his sense of touch burst into life. There it was!

All over the side of his jacket! He was horrified and disgusted, and a flashback of earlier events popped vaguely into his mind. He'd fallen against the bonnet of his car where some rotten swine had thrown up and was now wearing the remnants of somebody else's lunch! Aaaarrgg!!

Wearing your own lunch was one thing. Wearing a stranger's lunch was an entirely different matter, and Jackie gagged at the thought of it. He couldn't get the car's soft-top open quick enough. He would've taken a knife to it if he'd had one handy, but businessmen didn't carry knives, so he had to wait for the electric motor to open the roof in its own time.

He needed fresh air, fast. He needed to get away from the stink. First things first, he needed to get out of the car park and on to the open road.

He turned the key, and the engine of his BMW Convertible came to life with a roar. He crunched into reverse and swung out of the parking bay faster than his reactions could cope with, tearing the front wing of his car along the length of a nearby van in the process. He heard the noise and felt the slight pressure of the impact but decided to ignore it. The last thing he wanted to do was survey the damage he'd just done to his new car, let alone some heap of a builder's van. As far as he was concerned, it was too dark to see much anyway.

He slipped into first gear and rocketed out of the car park, totally unaware of the fact that the front passenger wing of his BMW now resembled an acutely deformed saw blade.

The West Port area was bustling with the usual Friday-night revellers. Appreciative Repertory Theatre audiences were quietly vying for parking spaces in South Tay Street, while swarms of student cliques shouted obscenities to each other in Latin as they filtered from pub to pub in search of stronger and cheaper alcohol. Flocks of clucking girls on a night-out. Bands of blokes acting brave to impress anything in a dress and making pure twats of themselves in the process. Freemasons en-route for downtown lodges, and Uncle Tom Cobleigh and all. The Friday night revellers were out in force. They were everywhere. Some of them were pissed drunk and couldn't give a toss, and some of them were pissed off at the maniac in the silver open-top BMW who drove up Old Hawkhill on the wrong side of the pavement at over fifty miles per hour.

The BMW was on autopilot. Jackie was on the horn. Luckily, he was still on the right side of consciousness. Just.

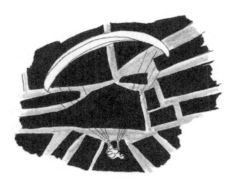

Iona loved the evening sky. She loved the whistling silence it offered. It was a place to retreat to when things were getting too much to handle, and the phone conversation she had at teatime with her patronising mother definitely fell into the 'too much to handle' category. She'd been soaring over the city in her new Competition Paraglider for half an hour and had calmed down considerably. The new glider was put through all the rigorous tests that she could think of, including the spit on the double-decker bus from 1000 feet test, and she considered herself lucky not to have been spotted yet. She knew she had to land sometime soon, so she narrowed down her landing site options to either Dudhope Park, which was slightly north of the Police Headquarters building or, one of the car parks at the West Port. The West Port seemed more attractive. It was just as close to the cop shop, but with more people around. She could mingle with the crowds and disappear into the background, no problem. She decided on the West Port. She'd tackle the Old Hawkhill car park this time round. It had a good chance of being half-empty at this time of night. Hopefully.

Jackie gripped the steering wheel and tried his best to control his lolloping head. He closed one eye and attempted to focus the other. He knew his turning was coming up soon and didn't want to over-shoot the junction. Like the drunken maniac that he was, he jerked the wheel hard right and turned the corner at thirty miles per hour.

Wondering what all the cars were doing parked in the middle of the road, he came to a sudden halt. It took a couple of minutes and a good few guesses before Jackie realised that he'd driven into another car park. It took a further couple of minutes and another good few guesses before he decided on a course of action, before he wet himself, and before somebody walked around the corner and into the car park.

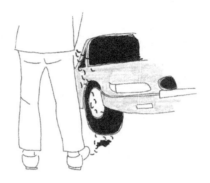

The relief was instant, and Jackie smiled in appreciation of the simple things in life. If only things were as simple and clean cut as having a pee on the wheel of your own car, life would be so sweet. So... simple!

Jackie's life was a messy tangle of complications and worries. His life was definitely not simple and clean cut. Nor would it ever be. His recent escapade with the prostitute and the snake had seen to that. It was the straw that broke the camel's back. The poke in the eye with a rusty nail. The kick in the shin. The dig in the ribs. The fart under the duvet. It was everything rolled into one. The funny thing was, if it hadn't involved a python, his wife might never have taken the kids and moved in with her sister. A solitary indiscretion with a prostitute may, in time, be forgotten, but sexual encounters with very large snakes were the stuff of legends. Especially when they're printed in kodacolour on eight by ten photographs and posted through your letterbox.

Iona turned her paraglider into the wind and prepared to land. She let go of her small rucksack and allowed it to dangle twenty feet below her on a rope that was secured to a karabiner on her harness. She liked the thought of having an additional braking system in the event of a last-minute gust of wind. She'd fallen foul of that before and been dragged a fair distance along the ground on many occasions. That was the bummer about landing in built-up areas. The trouble with wind is that it can be a right pain in the arse. And the knees, the back, the arms, and the ribs, if you're not careful.

Jackie never heard a thing, except for the roar of his engine, and a little voice inside his head saying, 'Get home as quick as you can! Alice and the kids are probably there right now, picking up the rest of their clothes! Hurry, get home now... they're right there! Hurry, before you miss them!' He heard nothing else. He was too busy heading for the car park exit. He never heard the rucksack falling into the rear seat of his car, or of it catching into the folds of the soft-top. He never heard the TWANG of the rope stretching tighter, as he accelerated out of his predicament. He never heard Iona screaming for him to stop the car.

Pity.

THE ROAD AND THE MILES

Navigating roundabouts can be a problem for a lot of drivers at the best of times, even well-seasoned drunk drivers with years of experience, and Jackie was no exception. He had three main problem areas. One, he was so drunk that he could fall from the top of a multi-storey without breaking as much as a fingernail. Two, he was hurtling his BMW towards the roundabout at almost sixty miles per hour. Three, twenty feet above him he had a screaming passenger in tow.

As a result of being heavily under the influence of problem one, Jackie never saw problem two until he was halfway across the roundabout via the direct route over the middle, and by that time he was beyond caring about it anyway. He was so deafly drunk and oblivious to his third main problem, that for the remainder of his life, his conscience would be clear. He would know nothing about it. Absolutely zero. He hadn't been privy to that kind of information, and never would be. He would know nothing about a happy-go-lucky sixteen-year-old who was slammed against a streetlamp at sixty miles per hour and strangled to death by the cord risers of her tangled paraglider. He would know nothing of the heartache and loss he had contributed to. His conscience, on this occasion, was clear.

The Lochee Road was also clear, and Jackie tackled it at high speed. He wanted to get out of the city and back to

Auchterhouse village, pronto. If Alice and the kids were home, he wanted to be there to see what was going on. See if she had that sister of hers with her. See if she was pulling the strings and persuading Alice to strip the house of all its contents and leave him with nothing.

His mind was racing faster than the BMW. His thoughts were ten miles north of his present position and already well into a shouting match with his sister-in-law. A shouting match in which no words were slurred, and all stops were pulled. A shouting match that he was winning and well in control of. Which is more than could be said for his driving.

Charlie stopped his taxi on a double yellow outside the Logie Club, hoping that his passengers would get out sharpish, so he could double back along Liff Road to the roundabout and pick up the fare that had tried to flag him down, before some other cabbie tagged them. He was having a good night and was greedily looking forward to the rest of it, if his luck held.
Life, however, can be a bitch sometimes.

THE ROAD AND THE MILES

Suzi had been teasing Lenny for most of the journey. She was the world's greatest flirt in Lenny's eyes, not to mention his breeks, and she knew it well. It was staring her in the face, and she knew that it was her who put it there. The lump in his suit trousers was definitely not a rolled-up Sporting Post. How he was going to get out of the taxi with one hand in his pocket, she never knew. She was too busy giggling. She was too busy having a good time. Too busy climbing out of her side of the taxi so she could run around the back and see the state of Lenny as he got out of his side. She was busy. Too busy. Her head was full. Of shite.

Pity.

The mobile phone had been ringing for ages and Jackie was in two minds whether to answer it or not. On the one hand, it was just the thing to keep him awake at the wheel, on the other hand, it might be Alice trying to get in touch with him. The only problem with answering the call was that the phone was in his jacket pocket, hidden behind a force-field of stranger's spew and Jackie retched at the thought of putting his hand anywhere near it. He decided to do what only a drunk can decide to do. He decided to slip out of his jacket, up-end it, allow the phone to drop neatly onto the passenger seat, throw the jacket on the floor, and pick up the phone. Simple. Or it would have been if he had unbuttoned his jacket first.

JOCK TAMSON'S LEGACY

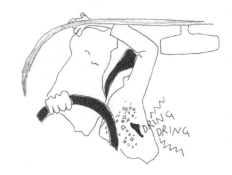

He was in such a state getting the jacket off that he almost smothered himself twice in the fracas. He'd drunkenly mistaken his jacket for a jumper at the crucial last moment and was momentarily swept up in the simplicity thing again. He began to regret the move during the initial struggle with his right arm. He was panting for breath like an asthmatic greyhound, and sweating like a malaria victim by the time his head was finally freed, and he was well pissed-off with the inconsiderate sod who was on the other end of the phone.

Jackie hated his jacket. In fact, he now hated all jackets. And jumpers. Right now, he hated jackets more, his especially. The one he was wearing. Was wearing. Will no longer wear. The jacket, which he threw to the floor with loathing and hatred. The jacket that had the mobile phone in the pocket. The jacket that was lying on the floor, staring up at Jackie, saying, 'Come and get me if you've got the bottle, you yellow-belly with diced carrots, you!'

Jackie snapped. He went for the phone like a wild animal. Like it was a wild animal. A wild animal that Jackie was in the process of battering to death on the floor of the car.

Jackie was busy.

So was the mangled front passenger wing of his brand-new BMW.

THE ROAD AND THE MILES

Suzi hardly felt it. She never even heard the 'Bang' as the back door of the taxi was ripped from its hinges. She felt as if a strong wind had buffeted her back into the taxi just as she was trying to step out. It was a feeling that she'd never experienced before. She lay with her head on Lenny's immediately flaccid lap. Something was wrong. She was aware of that fact. But she was caught in a daydream of trying to figure things out rationally as her eighteen-year-old body went into automatic shutdown.

The feeling that Charlie had in his water at the start of his shift was instantly, and irretrievably gone. So was the control he had over his bladder. The 'Bang' had seen to that. And the blood. Oh, the blood! He'd never get that stain off his upholstery!

Suzi thought that she was thinking rationally. Her oxygen starved brain, however, was telling her different. It was telling her about good times and giggling with her lad on the couch one night when they were babysitting for Irene and Lenny. It was telling her about the time in Flipper's flat in Lochee... the time when they almost kissed for the first time and the chair broke and they ended up on the floor and Flipper's wrist ended up in plaster...

Her brain was telling fibs. Whoppers! In her head, at that moment, she was having a great time.

Lenny was definitely not having a great time. He was too busy screaming. He was too busy panicking. He was too busy trying his best not to look at all the blood. He was wishing that he'd went to the Pan Loafy Hotel with his wife after all, like a dutiful husband, instead of trying to get his hands inside his babysitter's knickers while her lad is somewhere in the Caribbean.

Unknown to Lenny, Flipper was no longer in the Caribbean. At that very moment, he was standing at Lenny's front door, having a conversation with Lenny's highly embarrassed and lightly oiled wife, Irene.

It would be hard to say who seemed the more desperate, Flipper or Irene. She was desperate for Flipper to take a hike, so she could get back to taking advantage of her husband's absence and back to the man she had shackled to the headboard of her king-size bed. He was desperate for a cuddle from Suzi. He was desperate to see her, to be with her and smell her, and be comforted by her. He needed sympathy. He was desperate for it.

If anybody needed sympathy it was poor wee Suzi. She'd lost consciousness as a result of losing so much blood after losing her right leg to the mangled front passenger wing of a silver BMW which was being driven at high speed by a man who was in the middle of a fist fight with a mobile phone.

At the moment of impact, Jackie had been in the process of silencing the annoying digital bleeping by pinning his mobile phone against the floor of the car, in an attempt to squeeze the life out of the inconsiderate bastard who was on the other end of the line. He never saw Suzi. He never even saw the taxi.

THE ROAD AND THE MILES

When he raised his head to look up at the road ahead, all he saw was a shoe. A woman's shoe. And it was caught on his windscreen-wiper blade. It was being buffeted by the wind and was attempting to dance along the windscreen to freedom.

Jackie turned his wipers on full and helped the still-warm shoe on its way.

"Little brats!" slurred Jackie, blaming the shoe caper on some local street kids who weren't even there.

It wasn't the first time something like that had happened on his way through Lochee. He'd had things thrown at his car on a number of occasions; condoms filled with watered down paint, plastic lemonade bottles, and snowballs... the usual stuff. He'd never had a lady's shoe lobbed at him though.

"Little toe-ragged fuckers!" he slurred to himself once more, and he floored the accelerator pedal to get out of the madness of Lochee as quickly as possible.

Ella's knee was giving her signals. By the time she'd arrived home from Canada, the itching had already stopped. Unfortunately, the swelling had started in earnest. Her knee had rapidly grown to the size of a FIFA-approved football within the past hour and was now grotesque enough to frighten small children at fifty yards.

Whatever it was that was going to happen, was going to happen soon, and it was going to happen to someone close to her, that she was sure of. Exactly when, and to which person, she still hadn't figured out. Her knee was never quite that specific with the details of impending tragic events.

She'd been home for almost an hour, and in that time, she'd phoned everybody on her friends and family call list to check that they were all right. They were. And that made Ella slightly edgy.

She made herself a cup of tea and sat by the living room window, looking with awe and dread into the darkening sky. She also looked with distaste and loathing at the car that had just parked on the grass verge in front of her house.

Mary didn't like the idea of parking her car on Liff Road, directly outside the pub. She was always a bit dubious about getting her paintwork scratched or her wheels peed on by some drunk. She did feel a bit guilty about parking on the grass verge in front of the houses opposite the pub, but she couldn't park too far away. There was all that Karaoke gear in the back of the car to think about. She didn't want Alfie to do himself a mischief with all the heavy lifting now that they had become an item once again.

Tonight's gig at the Whip Inn promised to be an exceptional and emotional experience for the Soul Lovers Karaoke Kruise and their entourage, especially after the goings-on at their mid-week gig for Mary's birthday. Tonight was a night not to be missed if you were a regular follower of Mary and Alfie's act. Tonight would be a night to remember. For sure.

Ella just couldn't let it go. She was hell-bent on giving the driver of the car an earful for parking their car on her bit of grass.
"Bloody cheek!" she muttered to herself, as she quickly shuffled down her front path like a re-modelled Frankenstein creation on amphetamines.
Alfie caught sight of Ella's approach and decided to ignore her. He knew she was about to give them a bollocking about the car, but the state that the old biddy was in, the only thing she looked like she would be able to catch was her breath. And besides, the karaoke machine that him and Mary were carrying wasn't exactly a featherweight toy, so he was in no mood for hanging around listening to tripe. He was in work-mode, and very busy with it.
Mary was trying hard not to snag her tights against the edges of the heavy flight-case. She'd already snagged a pair when her and Alfie were loading the car earlier in the day and had no intention of repeating her wee mishap during the unloading. She

hadn't shaved her legs in about a fortnight and there was no way in the world she would get up on stage wearing a pair of stubble-revealing laddered tights. Not tonight, not ever.

Mary was busy trying to protect her £1.99 tights, and she wished Alfie wasn't in so much of a hurry to get across the road.

Mary and Alfie were in the middle of things. They were in the middle of crossing the road towards the bollards, that separate traffic flow, when they heard Ella's blood-curdling scream, and they froze like a pair of chunky chickens.

Ella was just about to step out of her gate when she saw the silver streak out of the corner of her eye. Her knee flashed a jolt of electricity through her body and her brain recognised the scenario for what it was, the cutting edge of impending doom.

Ella's vision slowed events to a series of stop-frame animations, allowing her to analyse each frame at her leisure, and although the colours were a bit wishy-washy, she managed to pick out the details better than a sixty grand per year art critic.

She saw the silver BMW. She saw the mangled front wing. She wished she had her specs on to be sure, but she saw what looked like a leg, attached to the front bumper. She saw the young couple step onto the road. She saw the BMW accelerate. She saw the driver. He looked like he'd been dragged through a hedge backwards and was wearing a half-crazed smile. She saw him aim his car at the couple. She saw the drunken look in his eyes. She even saw the sleepy wee crusty that was lodged in his tear duct.

THE ROAD AND THE MILES

Ella heard the scream and the words, 'Watch oot!' but she wasn't aware that it was herself who shouted it out.

Mary and Alfie were lucky not to have been minced. They'd caught sight of the BMW when it was just inches away, and they both let go of the flight-case at precisely the same moment before leaping for their lives and falling on their arses.

The flight-case connected with the bumper at just the right height and, accompanied by a solitary leg, the case wobbled skyward in the general direction of the Big Dipper and beyond, before it wobbled its way down on-to the roof of Mary's bonnie wee car, where it opened itself up to the world and ejected an extremely heavy and very expensive karaoke machine out on-to the road, where it dispersed into a thousand fragments.

Ella was still analysing the frames. Even without her specs, she was now in no doubt about what she was seeing. The white thing that was flying through the air towards her was, as she suspected, a leg. A real human leg. It wasn't the kind of thing that was usually out and about Liff Road on a Friday night, and Ella couldn't help wondering who it belonged to.

The leg ran out of forward momentum and dropped from the night sky like the dead weight that it was.

Ella fell on her backside, trying to keep an eye on it. She was mesmerised by it when she should've been avoiding it. She watched it approach her frame by slow frame until it finally and brutally connected its shin against Ella's tightly swollen knee.

The pus that came out of Ella's knee was astonishing. Some of the squirts even reached as far as her next-door neighbour's moped, which was chained to the railings over thirty feet away.

Ella lay on her front path drenched in pus with a spare leg beside her. She felt relieved of the build-up of pressure in her knee, thanks to the spare leg, and she felt relieved that nobody was seriously injured, perhaps with the exception of the mysterious owner of the spare leg. Most of all, she was now relieved of the dilemma that had been haunting her thoughts for the past few days. She felt glad it was all over and things could get back to normal.

For Mary and Alfie, things would never be normal again. Their precious karaoke machine, their car, their coccyx, all smashed beyond repair. Their life was now in ruins and their nerves were now in a right state.

Alfie even adopted a stammer, and try as he did, he just couldn't get the word, 'Fuck' out for love nor money, and he knew as soon as he heard the drivel coming out of his mouth that his singing career was over. There was no room in the business for stammering nervous wrecks, no matter how much soul they had. Alfie, like his coccyx, was absolutely shattered.

Jackie was just as shattered, but he never had a problem with the word, 'Fuck'. He slurred it out loudly and with great ease. He was sorry that he missed the pair of them.

He'd been under the impression that Ella was in dire need of some assistance, and that Mary and Alfie were a couple of high cheekers who had just pinched something from the poor old woman. He thought he was doing his Good Samaritan bit and cleaning up the badlands of Lochee. He thought he was doing Ella a favour by trying to save her precious whatever-it-was from being ripped-off by a couple of shite-the-bed chancers. He thought he'd at least break the thieving little swine's legs.

Hence the word, 'Fuck'.

He missed them.

He blamed the booze for his lack of judgement. It was the first sensible thought he'd had for over a week, what with all the palaver about the snake and all, and he failed to realise it. He was too caught up in his irrational behaviour and his drunken irrational thoughts to have noticed mister sensible had reared his head to chip in his tuppence worth. He was feeling good. Brave. Invincible. Pished, yes, but hunky-dory with it. He was in the business of cleaning up the badlands and he fancied himself as the lone ranger.

"High-ho Silver..." he gibbered to himself, as he turned onto the Kingsway dual-carriageway. "...awaaayyy!" he screamed, flooring his accelerator pedal.

Robbie shifted his weight from one bum-cheek to the other. He'd been perched in the branches of his beech tree for almost an hour and had inadvertently starved one of his legs of its essential blood supply, leaving him with a left leg that felt like a lump of ox liver hanging from a butcher's hook. He would've given his leg a rub to help the blood supply along but for the fact that his left arm was also asleep, and he needed his right arm to hold on to the branch.

A breath-taking jolt of pain shot down his leg and into his boot, as his blood rekindled its relationship with his lower limb. He desperately needed to get to his feet and walk around for a bit but he just couldn't be bothered. He was twenty-five feet above the ground with a belly-full of home-made whisky and a thirst for the blood of a passing Dundonian. He was in the middle of his passage from boyhood into manhood and there was no way that he would allow something as petty as cramp get the better of him. He had a job to do. A Dundonian to shoot. It was a milestone he had to cross in the development of his ancestral beliefs and customs, and he was going for it big-time whether his arm and his leg were asleep or not.

He looped his high-powered .22 air rifle around his neck and gave his leg a brisk rub to get the blood flowing again, but it only made it worse. He had to get to his feet and there was no doubt about it. He had to apply some pressure to the numbed lump of useless flesh, which dangled lifeless from his hip before the thing dropped off of its own accord.

He briefly contemplated adult life as a monoped and saw himself selling newspapers on a street corner in the bucketing rain. It gave him the impetus to get off his backside and on to his feet.

It was a struggle, but he eventually made it. He slowly rose to his feet and grabbed hold of a branch that was just above his head.

That was when he saw the light.

Robbie froze in anticipation and watched the silhouette of the trees becoming more intense and defined against the dancing glare of the oncoming light. This was it! His crowning moment had arrived! All he had to do now was follow his instincts and he'd be a man in no time.

Without any concern for the poor bugger that was driving uphill towards him, Robbie kicked into combat mode and raised his rifle, only to find that his left arm was still having forty tingling winks and couldn't take the weight of the barrel. He tried to rest the rifle on a nearby branch, but the strap was still looped around his neck, and he almost launched himself out of the tree in the process. He resigned himself to the fact that if he wanted this particular Dundonian he'd have to do it with the help of only one leg and one arm. He'd heard the term, 'I can do it with one arm tied behind my back' before and laughed at the thought of doing it with one arm flopped in front of him.

"Fuck it!" he drunkenly spat to himself, "I'll take this trespasser with one dangle armin' behind my back, no problem!"

He was sufficiently inebriated to be bravely confident. He was strong enough to do it and crazy enough to try it.

And try it he did.

JOCK TAMSON'S LEGACY

The BMW rocketed uphill with precarious ease. Jackie had left the orange plume of city lights a mile or so behind and was heading North. The narrow twisting road that hugged the boundary wall to Camperdown Country Park was treacherous to say the least and Jackie was blissfully unaware of any potential danger. He was mildly hypnotised by the flickering shadows of trees, that loomed out of the darkness at seventy miles per hour and were gone as quick as they came. He was wide-eyed, slavering, and his thoughts were away on an expedition to a place where his body wasn't invited.

Time travel, according to scientific debate, is a long way away and probably impossible to achieve, but Jackie was doing it no problem. He was reliving the past without the additional effort of having to leave the car to do it, and he'd never read a scientific journal in his life. He preferred the Daily Mail and Sunday Post. Jackie was gone. He was out of his body and away with the fairies. He was off to buy a biscuit without a penny in his pooch.

Maybe it was just as well.

Robbie squeezed the trigger as soon as he saw the headlamps and waited for the car to start swerving. He hoped that it would do a somersault or two, or maybe even explode, but it didn't.

"Shite!" he slavered, squeezing off another round.

Missed again.

The BMW was gaining ground quickly. Robbie knew that if he didn't get it with his next shot, he could be stuck up the tree for hours, waiting for another Dundonian to come along.

"Oh, fir fuck sake!"

Another miss.

Robbie snorted up a big wobbly snotter and prepared to gob on the car as it passed below him. He let loose the wobbly with perfect timing and to his surprise it never landed on the car roof, it landed right on the driver's head.

"A fuckin' convertible!"

He couldn't believe his luck. He'd plant one in the back of the driver's head, no problem. Without the bright lights glaring in his eyes, it would be easy.

Robbie's right foot pivoted on the spot. Unfortunately, he'd forgotten about the problem he was dealing with prior to the car showing up, and his left leg stayed where it was and went into involuntary spasm. He reached out with his left arm to break his fall against the huge branch, but it crumpled uselessly beneath the weight of his toppling body, and his head smashed against the rough bark. He was knocked unconscious on impact. He was following in the footsteps of his ancestors.

He would've fallen twenty-five feet on to a tarmac road if it weren't for the high-powered .22 air rifle catching in the branches. He probably would've survived such a fall if he'd fallen. He'd no doubt have been picked up by the next car to pass and taken to hospital if he'd fallen.

Only if.

Robbie McNicol the Fourth followed in the footsteps of his ancestors and was hanged by the neck from a beech tree until dead, his high-powered .22 air rifle acting as a modern-day hangman's noose, snapping his fifteen-year-old neck as easily as it snapped a couple of nearby twigs. He never felt a thing.

Jackie felt rain. Either that, or he'd been shat on by a passing pigeon. Whichever it was he didn't want to dwell on it too much. He was too busy with the past to be bothered with the present. He was in the middle of shagging an eighteen-year-old prostitute with a python wrapped around his legs and he didn't want to pull himself away from it. He was too close to the tickly bit. On the other hand, something was telling him to put the roof back up because of the rain and the pigeons. He niggled himself into making a move, and he flicked the switch for the roof, trying all the while not to lose the thought of the hooker.

Too late. He looked into the prostitute's eyes once again, only to find that they had changed. So had the prostitute. She was now his sister-in-law, and she was threatening to tell Alice and the kids about his sexploits when in waltzed Hugo Edderington of all people and slipped Jackie's maniac sister-in-law an envelope full of cash.

THE ROAD AND THE MILES

Jackie snapped back into reality with a jolt and a couple of swerves, one of which involved slamming against the kerb on the other side of the road. The roof being at a forty-five-degree angle didn't help matters much, what with his foot being thrust hard against the accelerator pedal at the time.

The very second that he felt slightly compos mentis, he slowed down. By then he'd travelled the length of the road and was approaching the junction at Birkhill. It was probably just as well that Hugo Edderington had popped into his mind, or he might never have slowed down enough to catch sight of the end of the road.

Jackie concentrated hard on his driving as he passed through the Siamese-twinned villages of Birkhill and Muirhead. It was the last clump of populated area that he had to drive through, and he didn't want to be pulled over by a young, over-zealous village PC who watches 'Police Camera Action,' on a weekly basis.

JOCK TAMSON'S LEGACY

He took his time. He cautiously meandered. He still couldn't quite control his lolloping head and was losing another battle against an extremely heavy left eyelid, but he was confident in getting through without a hitch.

He meandered on.

The speedometer meandered on too. It meandered between fifty-two and fifty-three miles per hour.

Jackie never saw the meandering striped cat. It meandered around his front wheel twice, before tightly lodging itself against the roof of his wheel arch with its tail tucked neatly between the brake pipe and the shock absorber.

Jackie loved to meander. It was what the countryside was all about. That was why he'd moved out of the city and into the Sidlaw Hills. He loved the slow permanence of it all. Things took their own time in the countryside and Jackie felt he fitted in perfectly. He felt he belonged. Auchterhouse Hill was in his blood, and his food-packaging business, with its hectic schedule, failing profits, and numpty employees, was the last thing he wanted to have in his life.

As soon as he'd driven past the last streetlamp, he considered himself out of Muirhead so he put the boot down once more. Driving slow was harder for Jackie than driving fast, and the quicker he sped away from the thought of his work, the better.

The only thing was, he was thinking with the Malibu and his dick instead of his brain, and every time he tried to re-kindle his mental encounter with the prostitute, up would pop Hugo

Edderington with a fist-full of cash.

Jackie hated complications. His life was full of them. Right from the start there had been complications. His birth certificate stated that his name was John Tamson, his mum and dad called him Jack, his mates at school called him Jake, a few people during his teenage years called him Johnny, and now, most people seemed to call him Jackie. He hated being a 'Jackie'. At school, when he was Jake, any laddie that was called Jackie usually got the piss ripped out them for having the name of a lassie's comic magazine.

"Jake Tamson." He proudly declared to the steering wheel.

He wasn't entirely convinced by his own declaration.

"Jackie Tamson." He made it sound more like a question instead of his own name.

"John Tamson." He said, almost involuntarily.

He was a thousand yards from home and having a ninety-four miles per hour identity crisis. If his sister-in-law was in the car with him, she would no doubt tell him exactly who he was… a low-life selfish money-grabbing sexual pervert who deserved to be shat upon for the rest of his life. He was a nothing. A nobody. He was a drunken arse who was driving at ninety-four miles per hour with his eyes shut, his head slumped against the side window, and his mind struggling with the concept of who he was and what he had contributed to the world.

The BMW hit the ancient Oak head-on.

A local forester had planted the oak tree at the sharp bend in the road over one hundred and fifty years ago. His name was Jock Tamson.
 He was no relation.
 Pity.

CHAPTER 10

AND THAT'S A FACT!

The Saturday edition of the local newspaper brimmed with the usual tabloid snippets of news. The front page carried three storyless photographs, a large car advertisement, and four tabloid snippets... three of which were of national interest, continuing the story deep inside the depths of page two and beyond. The other, curiously lonesome, sixty-five-word news report was a local snippet, wedged between the lower and left margins, carrying a photograph showing flood damage in Africa, and a story about a cabinet minister accused of sexually molesting a dolphin while scuba-diving in the Moray Firth. The page one, local interest story carried the headline – *Birthday tragedy*. The sixty-five words included the headline word-count.

On the face of it, nothing much of consequence has been going on in the Dundee area of late, except for a tragic accident involving a fatally injured sixteen-year-old girl, who was left tied to a lamppost in the city's west end after a birthday prank went wrong.

Newspapers, as we all know, deal mostly in facts, not consequence.

Pity.

Deep inside the depths of pages four and five, lie the remnants of the local goings-on. The LOCAL NEWS pages. The meat and bones of the residents' political, criminal, and social gossip. Facts, and plenty of them. As usual, photographs dominate the pages and page four carried six large prints of various smiling groups bearing oversized cheques. None of the photographs were accompanied by more than two lines of text, allowing a plethora of tabloid snippets to be thrust upon the remainder of the page in a gaggle of information. Facts. Not consequence.

The consequence of Ella's encounter with the spare leg was explained away in less than two hundred words under the headline – *Lochee woman attacked*. The report dealt only with the facts. The police confirmed that a woman had been taken to Ninewells hospital following an incident where she was injured outside her home. A nameless neighbour whose moped was also damaged in the incident, confirmed that the sixty-eight-year-old woman had recently returned home from Canada. Two witnesses to the incident were reported as, smashing a karaoke machine nearby, and had seen very little of what happened. A report was being sent to the procurator fiscal.

Robbie's factual encounter with the beech tree and the high-powered .22 air rifle was summed up further down the page. It was economically headlined in three words, *Youth's body found*. The rest of the facts were concisely squashed to under forty words – *Tayside police have confirmed that the body of a youth was discovered late last night in the Birkhill area, on the outskirts of Dundee. The police spokeswoman told reporters that they were treating the fatality as accidental.*

Facts are facts after all, and the fact remains that two inconsequential, yet apparently accidental teenage deaths and an attack on a pensioner are factually reported on page four. If it's in print, it must be true. If it's not a fact, it's of little consequence to busy newspaper editors. On a daily basis, busy newspaper editors' shave straight through the furry bits surrounding a story to get to the juicy facts at the core. Who needs a long-winded report when a good headline and a few facts from reputable sources will do?

More facts, not consequence, were found across the page to the right, immediately below an optimistic article about the reduction of drink-related driving offences in the region.

Irene was relieved that her name wasn't mentioned in the paper. It was bad enough that half of Castle Park's residents were subjected to the breach of the peace. The other half no doubt, subjected themselves to the commotion through the twitching cracks of their vertical blinds. Fortunately for Irene, the editor of the local daily had a sister who lived in Castle Park and, fearing for the property value of his beloved sister's home, the editor shaved through the fur, bones, and guts of the report until only basic facts were left to tell the tale. The tale of basic facts was printed under a minimal heading declaring, *Police called*. Since the story had had its fur shaved off, its bones ripped out, and its guts bastardised, not many people would get to know about the ultimately unlucky teenage drug dealer who was severely set-upon by a highly-strung young mother wielding a four-foot long, hallway mirror. All anyone would know was the basic facts. Flipper, too, was glad that his name didn't show up in print. He had a reputation to uphold. Street cred to maintain. It wouldn't do for the whole city to know about the walloping he received about the head and body, or of the long blood trail he left as he ran away from Irene and the strange naked man in the handcuffs. Fact or consequence? Who knows?

Fact – The police were called to a breach of the peace in Castle Park. Fact – a young man was injured. Fact – a naked man wearing handcuffs attached to a velvet bedstead was seen running away from the scene. Fact – police are appealing for witnesses.

Facts are facts.

The guts, the bones and the furry bits surrounding the stories are of little consequence.

Pity.

On page five, the facts leap off the page in true tabloid style, circumventing any loose consequence and heading straight to the nitty-gritty via the headlines.

Poor Charlie. He got the bums-rush. And the biggest headline! The words stood one and a half inches tall at the top of the page. They were all facts, of course. *ILLEGAL PARKING BY TAXI-DRIVER CLAIMS THREE VICTIMS!* The two-thousand-word news article spread out beneath the headline like a plague upon all taxi drivers. The first paragraph, true to form, stuck to the facts. Two men and a young woman had been rushed to Ninewells hospital following a traffic accident involving an illegally parked taxi. The hospital has not revealed the identities of the crash victims. The police spokeswoman did say that a report was being sent to the procurator fiscal. It was unfortunate that the next eighteen hundred words lost the plot and began to drag up unsubstantiated scare stories of speeding cabs owning the roads, impolite cabbies swearing at their customers, and the dangers that young women face if they step into a taxicab alone at night. Underneath the article, a full-colour eight by ten photograph of the scene revealed Charlie's bloody, mangled, and doorless Ford Orion taxicab parked on double yellow lines outside the Logie Club. The caption below the eight by ten read – *A tragedy waiting to happen?*

Perhaps newspaper editors do occasionally buy into consequence after all! Then again, perhaps not.

Hugo Edderington's benevolent smile beamed out from the centre of page five as he received a monolithic cheque to the value of twenty thousand pounds from a grey suited group of elderly business types at a civic function in aid of the under-privileged jobless youth. The photograph was carefully set up to record the fact that something positive was being done to help under-privileged youths in Dundee. The photograph, (along with many of the original taxicab scare stories) had been set up by Hugo. It had been meticulously planned and executed in order that Hugo would be viewed by the voting public in the best do-gooding light possible. The caption below Hugo's feet dribbled out the facts – *Mr Edderington receiving a cheque on behalf of the Under-Privileged Youth Training Project*. The fact that most of the newly donated money had already been promised to a Mercedes dealership in Perth was of no consequence.

Pity.

Factual compression being at the forefront of tabloid journalism in general, and local journalism in particular, page five of the local rag contained a long, narrow column, crowned by the word – 'BRIEFLY', where more snippets of consequence were steadfastly reported as facts. Brief facts. Facts that were so minutely brief, they were almost molecular.

Road crash victim named, proclaimed one brief fact, leading in with the report about a well-known Dundee businessman, a family man and pillar of the community who miraculously survived after his car went out of control near his Auchterhouse home. The emergency services took almost three and a half hours to cut father of two, John Tamson from the wreckage of his BMW convertible. A Ninewells hospital spokesperson confirmed the fact that the victim had received multiple body and head injuries and that his condition was "serious".

The facts spoke for themselves. Jackie had survived. He was brain-dead and on a life support machine, lost forever in the mechanically induced limbosphere of medical purgatory uncaring of who or where he is.

Pity?

JOCK TAMSON'S LEGACY

EPILOGUE

The ancient oak was planted in the mid-19th century. It marked the precise spot where the first-born son of local forester Jock Tamson, was crushed to death under the hooves of a galloping thoroughbred whose rider was blind drunk on Birkhill whisky. The tree planting was attended by over fifty locals who, like Jock Tamson, spat twice on the ground beneath the sapling oak. One spit to place a curse on the drunken rider of the thoroughbred who killed Jock's bairn, and the other spit to place a curse on all drunken riders who may pass by the spot in the future.
There were no headlines to tell the facts. Or the consequences. Pity.

THE END

Printed in Great Britain
by Amazon

39028102R00073